The Secret
Testament
of JULIAN

The Secret Testament of JULIAN

by

Simon Parke

www.whitecrowbooks.com

Preface

When the anchoress Julian of Norwich died in 1416, she left two manuscripts, written in the small cell – ten feet by twelve feet - where she had spent over forty years of her life.

The first was *The Revelations of Divine Love* - meditations on the visions she received during a life-threatening illness, before entering her cell. These revelations were taken, hastily and under the cover of night, to Carrow Abbey. There they were copied and in time, a version was smuggled to France.

Julian's work remained largely unknown, before finding a wide readership across the world in the twentieth and twenty-first centuries. Her *Revelations* became famous both for their unique spiritual insights and for being the first book written in English by a woman.

Thomas Merton named her, with Cardinal Newman, 'the greatest English theologian'.

The second manuscript, however, was not treasured by the nuns of Carrow Abbey. Initially owned by Mr Thomas Bookman, who knew Julian, it came to light only when the church of St Julian was bombed during World War II.

Miraculously, the manuscript was saved from the flames and went again into private possession. But an edited version, translated from the Middle-English, is now published for the first time. The manuscript in question is a more personal account of her life and times, variously sweet and rough, wounded and free. Perhaps written only for herself, she lays her senses plainly before us. And she names it, *The Secret Testament of Julian*.

This is the book you now hold in your hand. Let Julian speak.

Part One

1

So I write from my prison. Or is it my palace? I know not. It feels like a heavenly palace today. Experience will decide.

And my first line is written, I can scarce believe it. There! I am quite free to write; it is hard to contain my joy.

I start simply and slowly, allow me this; I hope to reward your patience, for I do not like slowness myself. I will quicken, believe me!

And you will wish to know why a woman who loves the sky, the harbour and the bluebells, chooses to be walled in for life; enclosed in a cell, without exit and without light. I will explain myself. But I will explain in English, which even now I write slowly, without practice.

And I smile ... I smile at my writing desk. I may be enclosed, but I can barely say how free I feel behind these walls, as if all worries are quite melted, like icicles in the sun. Though some say I am dead.

The bishop declared me dead when he bricked me in; and my mother cried.

'Why do you do this to me, Beatrix?'

We will return to them, though both advise me not to write, I know this. I write wickedly. They say I should not turn my woman's thoughts, memories and visions into ink on a page.

'The devil laughs when a woman writes, it is well known!'

But I do not hear him at present. And anyway, let the devil laugh, if he so wishes; his mirth does not concern me; his hilarity is a broken noise. I do not fear him nor his gaunt-faced fiends, for they are fools; my visions made this quite plain to me.

And it is my visions which have brought me here. (Do you have visions? You must treasure them.) My visions changed my life and it is they which now make me a captive; but a captive by my choosing. For while I cannot leave, neither can others enter. And this is freedom for me ... to live with no accusing eyes.

I do anger at these thoughts, I will not pretend. Many men write of God ... Mr Rolle and Mr Hilton, and they write well, I read their work. Yet a woman, it seems, is gagged and ordered to be quiet concerning the kindness of God. Gah!

And my mother agrees it should be so; she agrees her daughter should have no voice ... when clear as a sunset in June, I have seen both God's goodness and his wish that it be known by my fellow Christians in Norwich, England's foremost town ... though some speak of London.

I am, of course, unworthy. I do not have the lettered voice of a celibate cleric, for I am neither; nor do I speak as a teacher of canon law ... I have not studied. And you will find little of the cloisters in my tone, little of the monk, friar or nun, for this is no catechism. But find here, if you dare read, an honest telling of my life and the meeting which changed its course.

And though unqualified, I am ready to write; quite ready ... I have here the tools. I have a desk where I now sit, my parchment is attached by iron clips; and under my desk, a wooden box holding quills and ink.

I will brew ink from crushed oak galls and rain water, aged with an iron nail. Sister Lucy taught me this. She knows a great deal about ink, and she will visit me here in my cell. She will be my spiritual director, straightening me; she says this must be so.

'I shall be your straightener' she says. 'To save you from crooked ways.'

'I do not plan on crooked ways, Sister Lucy.'

'No one does,' she replies. 'No one plans them; but all find them. They arise unbidden and quite unnoticed.'

'Then you must notice them for me!' I say gaily.

'And you will scream in this place, Julian.'

She says this, though the words seem strange; they make no sense.

'I am too happy to scream, Sister Lucy. Why would I ever wish to scream?'

She does not know me. And my writing ink sits ready, in a sea shell I found at the harbour, where my father took me often. Daily it reminds me of him, dry from sea slime, now fixed to the desk.

And my goose-quill pen, the gift of the vicar, Mr Curtgate, who worries too much.

'Are you sure this is what you want?' he says.

'I am most sure, Mr Curtgate. God has made it very clear.'

'You seem certain of God's voice.'

'Is that a sin?'

'Not a sin, no ... though sometimes mistaken.'

I am amused by his fears; they make me chuckle. And I have three such quills, as well as a knife, for sharpening and to scrape mistakes away.

The parchment which carries these words is scraped animal skin, dried, stretched and polished with pumice to remove the fur. This was my father's trade, the tannery. He said Norwich makes the finest parchment – goat, sheep or cow ... and I like it that even now, I touch the animal as I write, for planets, elements, plants and creatures - they work in their natures to the benefit of us all, and I bless them now as my quill scratches, for they hold my words and make Norwich famous with their fine wool. And has not wool paid for a church in every village in Norfolk? Yes, God bless our sheep!

'Norwich is best,' my father would say and truly, I was born into a busy city, the centre of life. The world comes knocking on our door here!

'You come from the commerce class,' he would say on our harbour walks, 'More closely tied to the Low Countries than London, a boasting city we need not!' And I am proud to be of commerce class, though for parchment, vellum from calf is better, I know this ... but I do not have vellum and nor do I have my father. He fades a little in my memory; I do not see him so clear now, and his voice is gone, though I wish him here. But I make straight lines across the page, with a straight wood; for my hand wanders without lines.

And the parchment is given by Mr Strokelady, who you will meet in a while. It is a gift I accept, despite events.

'I hear parchment is what you most desire, Beatrix,' he says. 'And so I will provide it. I care for you, you see?'

It is what I desire; but I do not desire it from him; truly, I wish nothing from him. He has not spoken of the past, or of things done; he makes no mention of them, as if they disappear with time; as if those things were never done ... as if I invent them.

But they were done, there is no invention; and there is nothing resolved with Mr Strokelady. Yet without coinage of my own for the parchment, I accept the gift ... or how can I write?

So let me welcome you to my small and perfect three-windowed world. You may come and go; but I am here for life.

And I feel so free.

*

My three windows ... I look at them now, curtained.

First, there is Sara's window, through which my food and drink shall arrive and my bucket of waste depart. Second, there is the Visitor's window, through which I will speak with those who seek counsel. And finally, to my right hand as I sit here, the cross-shaped squint into the church, the Christ window, through which I shall receive the mass and confession.

And I shall not be cold come winter, or only a little; for I shall build peat fires, as was our practice at home. The peat is a gift, though I know not who gave it; and I am told there is the promise of more. Norwich priory needs two hundred thousand bales of peat a year, drawn from the marshlands. I shall not need as much, there are sixty monks in the priory, more cold skin than here ... but I shall need some.

'The donor asks to remain a secret,' says Mr Curtgate.

'All gifts are from God, so there is no secret,' I declare. 'It is from God!'

'As you say, Mistress Julian ...we merely pass the treasure on.'

Parchment is more needful than peat, this is so; but you cannot write in the cold of February without the friendship of fire. I know this from the scriptorium at the abbey. Some nuns, those older in years, scribed with blue fingers; but I cannot do this. Thick fog and chilling winds arrive from the sea, enough to numb our Norwich bones. I will need the fire.

While outside my cell, there is a porch for visitors, safe from the rain; and a chair where they may sit, as they talk through the window. When they come to me, they can rest a little; I hope they find rest.

The bishop says I must build business, that I must counsel rich visitors, and hope for grateful legacies when they die:

'An anchoress must pray, counsel and make money. Or how else shall she live?'

I say she will live from God's kindness and he laughs.

But while visitors will come and go, I will remain. No more can I walk the streets, through Needles Row, Spicers Row, Ironmongers Row or my favourite, Apothecaries Row – the kindest smell in Norwich. Nor shall I hear French, Italian, Spanish, Dutch and German in the market place, fighting for place and price. The bread market, cheese market, flesh market, poultry market, herb market – the grocers, the fruiterers, fishmongers and egglers! How can I say goodbye to these? Yet I do ... and nor will I gaze, and here I sadden again, upon the wintry cathedral skies or swaying trees of summer's dawn. Visitors may come; but I must stay.

Though I do not escape the world, as some suggest. They call such walling in an escape.

'You seek escape from the world – but why? To avoid another marriage?! Was your first marriage so bad you must place walls between yourself and another?'

But I do not come here to escape the world; I come here to sit in its flow, like a rock in a stream, steady and anchored ... an anchoress. We must all make well of the prison life gives us.

But I will need a fire.

*

All is quiet in the city. Darkness has fallen, and I hear the dark ... it is somehow a sound. No one shouts at the apprentices ... the carts, the cursing and the selling have ceased. Norwich, my dear city, like a tired carpenter, lies at rest, beyond my three windows.

And I start to write and I start with my walling in.

I will write of this first - though where I will end, I cannot tell. Who knows beyond this day? 'Have anxious thoughts about nothing,' says St Paul - though anxious thoughts arise, despite his command.

Will my funds be sufficient? Will I be maddened by this enclosure, as some suggest? Will I miss the sun and the moon, now denied me?

I do not know ... but I will write from my tomb, knowing that Christ rose from his. And I will write things from here that I could not write beyond it; for I am secure in my hiding, when outside, no one is secure and no one free from judging eyes.

'I can still see you,' my mother would say when I was a child; I remember this. She stood elsewhere in the house, but said 'I can still see you.' And for many years I believed her. But she cannot see me now, sealed in by stone and mortar. And if you read these words you will, in time, know why I chose this grave. And perhaps, with time's passing, I too will better know.

*

I have not been hasty; neither will I be.

I have waited some weeks before starting to write; the ink sitting calm and the quills quite clean. I have wished to pray, to be safe, and to listen to Mr Curtgate through the squint. I learn structure from his sermons, more than goodness. This I have found. I learn how to explain a theme, rather than news of the goodness of God. It is the 'how' more than the delight which I discover in his preaching ... but this is gift. I do not need lessons in delight for I have had my fill.

And so now I begin, I learn to write by writing. And like a foal testing its legs, I use my own words. I no longer wish to copy the monks' Latin writings - other people's fine words in a language I do not know. I wish for my own words to speak of our courteous Lord and I will write sometimes ... I will not write always. I will not become a slave to this work ... but sometimes.

And I know people anger. Not all are pleased at my walling in, when truly I wish for their good thoughts. I do not desire their offence, but cannot help it. And the day itself, the day of the walling, was both terror and a joy, Bishop Henry standing outside my cell, reciting funeral words in the chill March air.

And I will tell you of it; and tell you of him. But even as my mother asked why, so might you.

'How come you choose this path, Beatrix – or rather, this end? For that is what it is. How come you choose burial at the age of thirty?'

Strong words, I hear them still.

So let me speak a little of my story; of the path that led me to this cell. Not each step was happy; and some were great pain to my feet ... though maybe each step was love.

I believe I forgive my past for not being more kind.

2

'Here comes my beaming Beatrix!' says my father, when I visit the tannery.

I am a happy girl, always curious, so I am told. And I try always to smile - for a smile is the best hiding for shame; and to please others, the best survival.

'Here comes my beaming Beatrix!'

And I like to beam and to make him laugh, I do that sometimes; and maybe also my mother, though she is not the laughing sort. The priest calls me 'Butterfly Beatrix', hopping from this to that, colourful and bright.

'You butterfly girl!'

This is how he speaks of me, and maybe I am so - I wish to be colourful and bright; though my task at home, ever since I can remember, is to take out the chamber pots and kitchen waste ... especially the fish.

And there is nothing bright there.

'Neither fish nor friar should overstay their welcome,' says my father ... and all of it carried by me, the shit carrier, to be cast into the ditch that passes down the centre of our street, a-buzzing with flies.

11

I do not mind. My friends think me badly treated, but I do not mind; I think of it as confession.

'You are never too young to sin, Beatrix,' the friar tells me. His sort, they prefer wrath over mercy. God's wrath, like strong ale, is always on their lips, with mercy for feast days – and even then, only a little. And so I imagine the waste as my shame, this letting go of all that is vile within - old fish, entrails and excrement, a quite wretched stench. Here is my sin, tossed into the ditch for the dung man to remove, to scrape up and carry away beyond the city walls to be cast into the river, the river Wensum. The boats may ride on that water to Great Yarmouth, but we shall not drink from there ... it would be an unkind solution.

And I think of Christ as the dung man, I see him as such, Christ the dung man, carrying away my shame - though my mother hits me when I say this, and tells me to mind my mouth ... or the priest will send me to hell, for how can Christ be a dung man? It is the greatest blasphemy and I am frightened. Though she misunderstands my meaning, which is the greater hurt; and I cry in my bedchamber, for my meaning is worship, the worship of our Lord ... she cannot understand.

Sometimes my father takes me to the harbour to watch the traders, arriving in their wherries from Yarmouth; or in boats from Sweden.

Sweden!

'One day, I will go to Sweden, father.'

'And one day I'll be king,' he says.

But still I imagine, I always imagine. At night, I imagine a land of great mountains covered in snow; wild men sending barrels of iron to our shores ... and vessels from the Baltic seas with scarred hulls, I watch them arrive. I hear of wintry waters with white-topped waves and freezing coves where fishermen break the ice; and I greet the herring, delivered for smoking, for pickling ... for reeking. They do reek, the herring ...

Ah, and Flemish lace! A different arrival, from Antwerp and Mechlin, and such delicate work. My mother says we can never have it, it isn't proper ... it isn't proper to wear such things or place them on our tables ... and Rhennish wine, now there's a sight, I have seen it poured, and it seems to leap and laugh - the colour of sunlight on the white cloth of the Mass.

*

My father dies in the plague – the first plague of the year of our Lord 1349, and it comes so quick, my mother's face a stone; a beautiful stone, but cold and unmoving and set against my tears.

'Is it wrong to be sad, mother?'

'We have no time for sadness, really no time. When travails come, we must get back on the horse, we must all carry on,' she says. 'No help in tears, no help at all. I do not need you tearful, Beatrix.'

I do not see my mother cry, though they say my father was a good man, kind to his workers at the tannery. He owned it, his life's labour, they say. And while my mother could have taken on the business when he passed - for the law allows a woman to own a company - she chooses against this.

'I will not do it.'

Instead, she sells it to Mr Strokelady, who owns the largest tannery in Norwich. He comes often to our house and she admires him; she speaks better of him than she did of my father. But I, Butterfly Beatrix, am less certain of his virtue.

*

The plague changes everything in Norwich with nothing the same.

It arrived in the year of our Lord, 1349, when I was seven. By the year of our Lord 1352, three quarters of the population had been taken, stacked high and untidy in the streets. I remember the piles - corpse upon corpse, they became familiar and not even cause for a glance.

How can this be? How can awfulness cease to be of note? How far this grand city is fallen!

Pope Clement in Avignon puts himself in seclusion. He surrounds himself with large fires, even in summer; and while his court dies around him, we hear from traders that he survives. So now all become popes and light fires around themselves. But my brothers do not survive, both older than I, black swellings the size of a fist in their necks, and somehow no time for goodbyes. My mother says we have no time, and it is true ... no one has time for the dead, or the bodies in the river. We attend to the living, those newly infected, though we run from them more, a red cross painted on their door.

The physicians prescribe the burning of dry wood, like juniper, ash, laurel, musk or cypress. They tell us to soak our floors in rosewater and vinegar, and drink potions of apple, lemon and peppermint. They advise all to shun sexual union and sadness - for these both strain the body. Yet having done such things, as money allows, still we die, and no physician in sight, too busy with their plans to leave.

Life is both simple and stark. When the plague comes, the only thought is 'Who will go next? My neighbour or myself?' "Two will be in the field and one will be taken."'

In the end, they dig burial pits outside the city, the grave yards over-filled - and God has no favourites. I was told only foreigners would die of the 'morte bleue'; we thought it a punishment for the French, so said our bishop at Pentecost.

'It is God's French blessing! And may they be much blessed!'

But I hear of monasteries, once full, reduced to a single monk. A single monk! Can this be believed? And while Carrow Abbey fares better, for women are stronger, many nuns are taken. Were they too such sinners?

And there is no market in Norwich; the market dies too - when the market, in truth, is the city! No traders from foreign parts, no chatter and no selling, a hollowness in our heart, like in the time of Noah. It seems a terrible judgement, a plague instead of a flood. And many name it a judgement, which further darkens our mood.

I feel shame that I survive, when my brothers do not ... when godly nuns do not, for I am not godly. I feel shame every day, and my mother looks on me in like manner. Perhaps she feels my brothers' loss, and finds no comfort in me. Perhaps she liked them more, I feel this too. And I am wary of illness, I even imagine it now. I feel sickness in my body, and believe and fear the worst; a slight pain and I imagine I shall be dead in the morning.

It seems certain.

*

Only slowly does life start again. Only slowly, and with difficulty, does spring come - like a sapling caught too soon in the frost; withered, deformed but alive, this dear city, opening again; a people broken and neglected, now coming alive.

'Mr Strokelady can help us,' says my mother. 'He is a man of means and famous in the city. God has blessed him in the tanning trade.'

So after my father dies, Mr Strokelady visits our home, to speak business with my mother. They close the door. He is also kind to me, bringing me gifts.

'You must look more grateful,' my mother says, though I do not want gifts from another man, standing in my father's space, resting in his chair. I do not want another man in that place.

But still he scoops me up in his arms and demands I visit his tannery.

*

'We stink with success, little girl!' Mr Strokelady tells me. I am overcome with the reek of caustic dye, like a knife in my nose, and choking. 'And success is a stink I can endure!'

William Strokelady dries hides, strokes his beard and sometimes strokes me.

'I am concerned for you, Beatrix, you must know this.'

'Thank you, sir.'

'I must look after you now, your mother wishes this; a young girl with no father.'

'I will always remember him.'

'Of course, of course.' He is flustered but smooth and wears fine scent. He smells the best of anyone I know.

'A decent man, we thought, a decent man - though caught in judgement's net.'

'I will always remember him.'

'But we cannot *touch* a memory, this I must say.'

He places his hand on my shoulder.

'I believe it can touch the heart,' I say. 'As does the memory of our Lord who we touch in the Eucharist.'

'But I can touch your body, Beatrix, as your father would wish.' I do not know if my father would wish this. 'We can play nice games together, we can play at touch ... if you wish your mother to keep her house.'

But his games were not nice, with his busy pushing fingers.

He sends hides overseas, with enough leather sold and coins counted to rip out his shutters and place glass in his windows. He shows me his glass.

'I don't show this to everyone,' he says. 'I reveal it to special little girls. What do you think of my glass, Beatrix?'

And though I like him not, it is here, in his home, that I first know a cleaner air, a scented air; an air without fish. His house stands near the river, where all the merchants live, the moneyed sort, and they breathe a different air. Until this day, until this moment, I have not realised such air exists, air so free of stain. I had thought all air stained ... though he will stain it, in other ways.

I look back now and feel only the stain.

But my mother liked my visits to Mr Strokelady. She said that one day he might be mayor; and when I told her of the glass in his windows, she liked him all the more, and told me to behave and to do as he bid.

'A man with glass,' she says, 'is a man you can trust.'

But I do not trust his fingers, which like my flesh too much. He touches against my will, placing me on his lap, and rubbing; and then easing me back, in the room upstairs, exposing himself. He speaks of a game, his face reddening as he does, but - I pause now, I cannot write of it.

And I do not speak of it. It is best not to speak, for my mother says he is kind.

'He puts food on our table, and gives us standing. He keeps us in our home.'

And this is true; I do not question my mother, it is not my place; I wish to help. I wish her to love me. And so while he visits and spends time at our house, I speak nothing of my visits to his; my mouth sewn up like a wool sack, for I know he buys her clothes.

'There are few women who do not possess something from Caen or Calais, Beatrix, really very few.'

'I believe I know some.'

He speaks as though all are rich.

'But table cloth and linen from abroad are everywhere, my dear girl, filling every closet! Women are everywhere decked in the trimmings of the French matrons, I see them every day in their glory. And if the continental matrons are sorrowed by their loss, then at least the women of Norwich rejoice!'

Though the nightmares come, and a distressed spirit. It is as though my spirit dies, its livingness eased out of the room and lost to view.

'Where is the butterfly gone?' asks the priest. 'Where is my lovely "Butterfly, Beatrix"?'

But the butterfly he knew is now heavy-winged, and prays to die. I ask to suffer unto death; to know the pain of our Lord on the cross and the suffering of his mother Mary, for the fiends come every day with their jabbering - and what else but such suffering can save me from my shame?

'You shouldn't tempt me, a most wicked girl!' Mr Strokelady says, and the words sink deep within, and find there a ready home.

I feel only shame and pray for the pain of Christ and for the wounds and the suffering of St Cecelia ...

*

I tell no one of these matters, excepting Richard; though only after we are married; I did not think it wise before.

We met at the harbour, where the boats sit with scarred hulls, awaiting redemption and mending. His father is a boat carpenter, Richard's trade as well.

He makes such beauty from wood, and joints of such strength, and we marry at eighteen, at St Julian's on King Street, just off Southgate. It is the smallest church in the city, but large with our happiness. It is a most joyful day with Mr Curtgate presiding. We are his first wedding, for he is barely older than ourselves, which my mother notices.

'A priest should not be quite so fresh from his mother's breast.'

But eleven years after the death of my father, the wedding is a day of hope, the colour of gold in my memory, even if Mr Curtgate did make errors, unable to say the word 'solemnly'. But we cared not ... not at all, there was nothing could dampen the day, not even the rain, for we were in love and beginning again.

And I did not plan to speak of Mr Strokelady, not to anyone, believing it better kept to myself. But while he has not touched me for a while – he stops inviting me to his house – I cannot always enjoy my husband in the bedchamber, which troubles him.

'I should tell you about a man,' I say, for he is very sad.

We live in two rooms in Peter Street, which we rent from Mr Strokelady.

'Which man?' he asks, and I believe Richard is angry for a moment, as though I have been unfaithful to my vows ... and truly, that is how I feel, the shame has not left this wicked girl, but slithers like a snake into everything I do.

'Mr Strokelady used to touch me.'

'I do not understand.'

And so I tell him of my visits to his house, and he says he will kill Mr Strokelady; and that I am never to talk to him again, and he will burn down the home in which we sit, being Mr Strokelady's property. I say we must know our place for now, not wishing to disturb my mother nor the agreeable rent we pay.

And soon after, I become large with child, which excites him; and indeed the both of us, though perhaps Richard the more, for he wishes for a son; and when Lettice is born, I grow into love, I grow into motherhood, knowing nothing like it, a quite unexpected sense - for this tiny girl is the fruit of Richard and me. Lettice is in some manner the three of us, the three of us are one and the three of us are a happiness I have not known. I cannot believe such gift nor blame her for anything.

'You'll discover she cries at all hours,' my mother warns me, seeing my joy. 'And then you might not be so pleased.'

But I do not mind her wailing, and cannot blame when she breaks the pot, for she is my child and Richard loves her too, and makes for her a boat from wood, rounded and curved, which he places in her cot.

'One day, Beaty, we shall all sail us to Sweden!' he says, for we have both heard tales from the merchants. 'In a boat just as this. And I will build it!'

But he does not build it ... such joy is denied. He is well in the evening, and laughing; we sing Lettice to sleep and listen together to the wind. He makes up a song to the creamy-white moon and then we lie together. But the swellings come in the night. I hear his discomfort, he begins to ache and groan. By morning, they are as chickens' eggs beneath his armpits and around his parts, the plague-boils, and I beg him to survive, he says he will, and I give him the boat to hold.

'You must take us to Sweden!'

'I will take you to Sweden, Beaty. And I shall build the boat.'

But the swellings are large and soft, full of blood and pus.

'You must pierce them!' he says.

'I cannot do that.' I wretch at the idea; really, I cannot do this. 'We need a physician.'

'There's no physician still here, for where's the money in the plague?' He laughs but speaks angrily in his pain, for all folk hate the physicians, with their leeches and star charts. They are scorned in the market place. 'They all go north to escape the plague and fill their purses. They have forgotten Norwich, so it has to be you, Beaty - now get the knife.'

It is true. People do travel north, everyone speaks of this. Even the king's physician, Master Gaddesden, has left London, finding refuge in Eltham Palace with the king.

'Wouldn't mind going north myself,' says Mrs Aske at the bakery. 'But then how would we live? Does the north need more bakers?'

They do say the north has cleaner air. They say only north-facing windows should be opened ... but no windows help us. Shutting my eyes, I pierce the boils, blood and pus oozing, black and yellow, a terrible stench; but no relief for Richard, who can only gasp and scream ... and then the vomiting begins, all that is in him coming out, dear Richard spilling himself on the bed. No priest will come and our neighbour closes her door, shrieking at me.

'You won't bring the plague to this home, you sinner's whore!'

I send word to my mother to come and take Lettice to safety, and she arrives well-covered, but will not enter. So I take Lettice outside, handing her over, and my mother takes her. She does not speak, her mouth covered, but nods and leaves, believing this to be God's judgement. She does not say this, she does not need to, for she spoke clearly when my father died.

'Where there is judgement, there is reason for judgement ... that is all I say.'

And the bishop agrees. He says we must root out Jews and heretics of the faith, that he will leave no stone unturned to purge Norwich of such demons, the cause of God's anger.

The flagellants had come in the spring, arriving from London. The bishop was not pleased, but the people cheered. They said they would save us by taking on themselves the sins of the city.

'The flagellants will protect us,' says my neighbour.

They come in their white robes, dragging a large cross down the street. And then stripping to near naked – only cloth around their parts - they march single file through the streets, chanting and whipping themselves and each other; and then falling to the ground, they stretch cross-shaped across the road in Ironmongers Row.

Each carries a scourge with three tails, for Richard finds one later; and each tail has a knot which holds a nail. He waves it at me in the street, laughing.

'Put it down,' I say.

'You don't like the nails?'

'I do not like any of it. It's blasphemy,' I say ... though I whip myself daily within with my thoughts.

'But if it saves the city?' he asks, and then laughs again, because he does not believe it will, and reckons it all a nonsense. He examines the scourge further as we walk home. Each tail is covered in blood and human sinew, where they have ripped into the flesh.

'Nice piece of work,' he adds, admiringly, for Richard likes things well made, even a scourge.

In the evening, the flagellants retire to their lodgings, to repeat the ritual the following day, and the day after ...though it seems our sins remain.

*

Richard is turning grey before my eyes, his skin turns, and he tells me not to look at him – 'Don't look upon me, Beaty, you must not look!'

Some say an aerial spirit escapes from plague eyes, striking anyone who gazes on them; though I cannot help but look, for he is dear to me.

'I must look, my love,' but I hear no reply, for his last words are spoken ... one does not know at the time. His last words told me not to look at him; but his eyes die mid-afternoon and his body soon after, gone in half a day, his body now blue, dismal in form, twisted and ugly, drained of life and taken from me, taken from Lettice.

I have seen bodies before, too many to note, but never the body of my own, dear Richard, holding the boat. He has let go of life, but will not let go of the boat. It is the boat that shall take us to Sweden.

And then Sara is at the door, shaking her head, holding a baby; I know it is Lettice.

'Beatrix!'

'Give her to me.'

'It shouldn't happen, mistress.'

'Did you find a priest?'

'Not one alive; and those that are alive are not willing.'

'Young Mr Curtgate will come.'

'He is in other homes, Beatrix; he cannot divide himself.'

I take Lettice, I unwrap her; she is a ghost, a pale face fading, cold as a winter stone, whiter than a lily, perfectly shaped and formed, her skin all a-chill.

'My baby.'

'Don't kiss her, Beatrix.'

I kiss her coldness, I can do no other. I press my eyes against hers and hold her to me.

'Where is Richard?' asks Sara.

I nod with my head to the bedchamber. Sara goes through and screams; I have not warned her.

'My God!' She comes to me again. 'May the saints save us!'

I walk back and forth, rocking my child - Sara tells me this, I don't remember. And she stays with me that night. I cry and I cry, the bodies laid out on the bed, side by side, so small and so large, a candle burning by their side.

'He won't let go of the boat,' she says. 'Why does he not let go?'

'We were going to Sweden.'

'To where?'

'You must leave, Sara,' I say. 'There is danger here, you know this. I have nothing now, but you ...'

'You won't be rid of me.'

'I will be rid, Sara, for I wish a long life for you.'

'I'd prefer a happy one.'

'And this is happy?'

'I'm happy with you, mistress.'

'I am not your mistress.'

'I serve your mother only to serve you.'

'Then you deserve better ... a great deal better.'

I give up my persuading. I give up all things beneath a clear sky, full of stars, for all things are taken from me this day, in less than a day, between sunrise and sunset, all is gone; and I hope for death. If fortune is kind, even now the plague boils ready themselves within me; this is how I feel.

'I'll ask Mr Curtgate to take the funeral,' I say.

I think ahead, it is less pain to leave this now. It is easier to make a plan, some future thing, than be here in this place with myself. I cannot bear myself.

'At St Julian's?'

'I wish them to be buried at St Julian's, yes ... where we were married.'

3

Richard and Lettice were taken from me in the year of our Lord, 1362, though our Lord seemed absent, the silence quite deafening; and I cannot now listen in church. I see only wall paintings of hell - the judgement, the screaming, boiling oil and so on. I see only adulterers stripped and spiked, grinning devils ... and Christ quite unmoved and unconcerned.

Can this be so? Is Christ unmoved by this turmoil, this plague, this ruination of our lives, this dread?

And in the street, so many hoods, differently coloured – Greyfriars, Blackfriars, Whitefriars and brown Franciscans, attached to monasteries but free to roam, to teach, preach on street corners, and to tell us of our sin, of our wasted and dreadful lives.

'Found wanting in the divine scales – so we are, so we are!' says the dribbling Father Jacob.

And, as if they are right - and God does rage and snarl like a wounded bear - this year brings also the storm. It is an upheaval of unimagined power ... savage, howling winds and water across the wet lands, the Brode water, surging in awful waves from the sea, farms flooded, barns washed away and families drowned in their beds; the fit and the fortunate climbing trees to live. Yet still I hear no comfort, no kindness in the preaching; and I worry for myself, how hard I have become, for I care for nothing.

'Am I now unreachable?' This is my thought.

I move back to live with my mother, no easy move. She continues in friendship with Mr Strokelady and makes herself busy running the home, telling me to be chaste if I seek another marriage. I am not to use lotions on my body or toss my head or shake my shoulders when I walk, lest men turn their heads and give me reputation. Nor am I to yawn too wide, laugh too loud, nor attend wrestling or cockfighting. I am not to enter a tavern nor answer a man on the street, lest people say I flirt or call me vain or name me a whore. But neither am I to delay.

'Men will not want a woman past her twenty-fifth year,' says Mr Strokelady, and my mother nods.

So when able, I take myself away to Carrow Abbey, where no men prowl; and I help in the kitchens, and listen to their chanting through the walls.

'I make myself useful,' as my mother would say, in the washing of pans and preparation of turnips; though I visit also the scriptorium, where texts are copied in Latin for the library. I peep through the door, I like the smell, the manuscripts and the ink ... and I enter.

And here is another world. Ah, reader – believe me, another world!

'Have you learned to write?' asks Sister Lucy, approaching me. She asks straight questions.

'I have learned a little, but wish to learn more.'

'And your Latin?'

'My Latin?'

I do not know what to say. I do not wish to be barred from this place, for it feels like heaven; but one must tell the truth.

'You will need Latin,' says Sister Lucy.

'I do not know Latin.'

'You do not know Latin?'

'It is not much spoken in the market.'

Sister Lucy, perhaps five years older, rolls her eyebrows in knowing surprise.

'Then how will you write, Beatrix, if you do not know Latin?'

'I can copy what I see; I need not understand.'

These days, I wish almost that I did not understand; for what I do understand brings sadness and fear.

'I will teach you Latin,' she says.

'I do not wish to learn it,' I answer, surprised at my firmness; as is Sister Lucy I believe.

Though I prove a good copier at Carrow Abbey; I learn the letters well. And sometimes, more privately, I write simple words to Richard and Lettice and place them on their graves by the oak tree at St Julian's.

'My world is cold and empty without you, dearest ones.'

Young Mr Curtgate takes the funeral ... Sara standing with me throughout the service, after which she takes me home and makes rabbit stew.

'My son is a clever lad,' she says. She indicates he has caught the rabbit; though on whose land it was killed, I do not ask. There is much hunger these days, with failing crops, rain upon rain and high prices. 'And if the rich can eat well, then why not the rest of us?'

I have not heard her speak in this manner. I nod in agreement.

'Mr Strokelady will keep you from hunger,' she adds, which makes me feel ill. 'What's wrong?'

She sees my face.

'I gave my thanks to Mr Curtgate,' I say, wishing to talk of other things.

'You will love again, Beatrix,' says Sara. 'Many do, the plague makes it so. It ends love and begins it again.'

'I do not wish to love again, Sara.'

'You say that now.'

'I will always say it. I have no more a place on this earth, I died with them. Your kindness melts me; but I am a stranger here.'

Sara looks at me, her face shocked; though my thanks to Mr Curtgate are sincere. He led the service courteously, performed without rancour or fear. He had named Richard and Lettice as children of God and named the plague as 'this stealer of life, this killer of kindness.'

Afterwards, he laid Richard and Lettice together in the ground, by the oak tree; boxes large and small, one on top of the other. And I feel taken there too, lowered deep into the ground, swallowed by the earth, beyond the reach of the sun; for we three were one heart, and how can a part-heart now carry on alone? I near jumped into the hole, to be with them; but, sensing such thoughts, Sara held me close.

'You stay with me, Beatrix. We will pass this way together.'

My mother is later displeased with Mr Curtgate, reflecting sternly on his sermon.

'I just wonder at his words.'

'Which words, mother?' for I had heard only the behovely kind.

'I just wonder how the judgement of God can be the stealer of life and killer of kindness?' she says. 'That I do wonder.' She does not shout, her anger held as tight as a tourniquet within, though filling the room. 'Those were his words, I believe. He called the plague the killer of kindness.'

'He sees what the plague does, mother. It rips at love.'

'But he does not ask from where it comes, Beatrix ... which is lack, I believe, a great lack. He forgets judgement.'

'The plague kills kindness every day, mother - it destroys folk, and hardens their souls.'

It has hardened mine and my voice will not be quietened, which frightens me, especially with my mother.

'I shall speak with him,' she says. 'It need not concern you.'

'It does concern me, if you believe father to have been a sinner.'

'Your father is dead.'

'And if you believe Richard and Lettice to be especial sinners, chosen for their wickedness. Is this why they were taken?'

'Beatrix, I have no wish to upset you; really I do not. But we must presume God's omniscience in this matter or what remains? Do you not listen in church? Now – there is cleaning to be done ...'

She does not like such discussion, sniffing at my question through her beautiful nose. She is still a beautiful woman.

'And Mr Strokelady ... he is a good man?' I ask.

'Mr Strokelady?' she says, as if she has scarcely met him. 'Why do you speak of him?'

'I see him here a great deal, so I wonder if he is a good man?'

'He lives, does he not?'

4

'You will need to understand ink,' says Sister Lucy in the scriptorium. 'You can't always be asking others for help.'

'Sister Rachel helps me.'

'And Sister Rachel is gone.'

'Oh?'

I am surprised, for she was here last week, and said nothing. It is Sister Rachel who had helped me the most. She has been kind when much else in my life is not.

'Where is she gone?' I ask, not wishing to lose her. 'Has she died?'

'In a manner.'

'In a manner?'

'She has become an anchoress nearby. It is a death ... though a living death.'

I have heard of such people, though I do not consider them much. For that is not my way. They take a vow of stability of place, sealed in their cells, 'like one sealed in a tomb', says Lucy. I cannot imagine it for myself; I like the sky and the harbour too much.

'The anchoress is buried, as one who is dead.' Sister Lucy does not sound pleased. 'It is a right calling for some.'

'And is it right for Rachel?'

'Who can say? There are some as go mad. And really, we cannot afford to lose nuns at Carrow. The plague leaves us sparse. A few more hours in the scriptorium, Beatrix, and you will be our abbess!' I blush.

I blush. 'I do not wish to be so! I cannot even lead myself.'

'Well, that is the hardest calling, so be not ashamed, and we shall hold Sister Rachel in our prayers.'

'We must do that. It must be fearsome to be buried alive.'

The thought becomes ever more dreadful.

'Nor can she help you with the ink anymore.'

And so Sister Lucy teaches me about ink, and the making of it; and of quills, and their sharpening and their care – 'that they last well and are not quickly thrown away. Ducks need their feathers as well,' she says. 'We cannot forever ask them for more.'

Though I believe she is concerned also for the Abbey's finances. The treasurer is a difficult woman. I have met her in the kitchens, demanding less for everyone. They say she is hard to keep content and rages over the quills.

'To copy a book - it is like a giving birth,' I say to Sister Lucy. 'Though to someone else's child and not my own.' I try not to think of Lettice. 'I copy the words - but they belong to another.'

'And that makes you sad, Beatrix?'

'I do not believe I am sad. I just observe that I am not the true mother.'

'You sound sad. Perhaps you wish that you were the mother?'

'I hardly say so!'

'Perhaps you wish the words you write were your own, Beatrix?'

'My own? And what have I to say? I have nothing to say, and less with every passing year; no words at all ... and no Latin in which to speak my nothing!'

And so there in the scriptorium, when I am finished in the kitchens, Sister Lucy teaches me to write and to make books of other people's words ... other men's words, the scriptures and the Early Fathers.

Though some while later, Sister Lucy draws me aside in the kitchens.

'I believe we have a manuscript which might be of interest,' she says.

'Why would that be so?'

'She's called Bridget.'

'A woman writes?'

'Bridget of Sweden.'

I think of Richard, and the journey he proposed. 'We shall sail to Sweden!' he said.

'I cannot speak their language.'

'The manuscript is in Latin,' says Sister Lucy.

'Then I am no nearer her than before.'

'But maybe you could draw nearer.'

'How so?'

'If you were to come to my cell after Lauds, I could read her meaning to you. From the age of ten, she had visions.'

'Visions? What sort of visions?'

'She saw Jesus hanging on the cross ... and asked him who treated him in this manner?'

'Bridget spoke with our Lord?'

And something inside me jumps, as if I am with child once again.

*

35

I remember also the shocking Mr Ball. He is set in my memory like a marking chiselled in stone. He speaks like no one I have heard before; and offends in equal manner. Mr Strokelady calls him 'the crazy priest from Kent' and says he will not live long. They all mutter about him; they call him a 'hedge priest', by way of insult, 'because only the hedges listen to him, since he was evicted from his church!'

'I now lecture sheep!' says Mr Ball, he makes a jest of it - though many Christians, the poorer sort, join the sheep and come to hear him in the fields.

'He sees peasants and nobility as alike,' says Mr Strokelady, 'as if they are quite the same!' He chokes with disgust into his wine, and my mother agrees, for she tends to agree to his face.

'Not even Beatrix would be fool enough to give him hearing,' she says, and casts me a look.

'Is he a fellow Christian?' I ask.

'He claims there was no nobility in Eden!' says Mr Strokelady. 'Neither kings nor gentlemen!' And then with a snort, he adds, 'As if Norwich is Eden!'

'Perhaps we should make it so!' I say, for it sounds a good call but my mother frowns. When we are alone, she tells me not to embarrass her in front of Mr Strokelady.

I do not tell them that I have heard Mr Ball myself. I do not to speak with Mr Strokelady, and avoid him when I can. And I have learned to stay quiet with my mother; there is no help in conversation. She will only find fault in Mr Ball; and perhaps I should too. He disturbs me, this I know. And I did not seek him out, I cannot be so accused. I did not seek him out, yet he sought me! He was there in the field by the abbey as I walked home, a desperate gathering around him.

'It is the wanderer!' one says to me, in much excitement, as though it is our Lord himself. 'The mad priest of Kent!'

He is a small man, and thin of build, but contains much force in his speaking; I have to stop and listen, for he is different from the friars.

'Why are those whom we call "lords", masters over us?' he asks. 'Can anyone here tell me? Why some are masters over others? No? Has Norwich lost its voice?!'

He makes great play of listening to the silence and some nervously laugh.

'Then let me ask again, in case you did not hear, the wind taking my words or perhaps your empty belly: why are those whom we call "lords", masters over us?'

This is how he starts.

'How have they deserved it, my friends? I ask this - and perhaps you do too? By what right do they keep us enslaved? For when Adam delved and Eve span, who was then the gentleman?' There is more laughter, though awkward, unsure if it is allowed. 'From the beginning, all men by nature were created alike, this is surely so? Our bondage and servitude came after – and not from God but from haughty men, who seek to oppress, to sit on our backs with buckled boots and beat us with sticks. We act like their slaves, yet we are not their slaves! We are descended from our first parents, Adam and Eve, who had no titles or airs. So how can they say they are now better than us?'

God forgive me, but I cannot help but listen.

'Brothers and sisters, gathered here in Norwich, we are all created equal, are we not? If God willed that there should be serfs, he would have said so at the beginning of the world.' He would have said, "Let there be serfs – especially in Norwich!" More laughter and louder now. 'But no, we are formed in Christ's likeness, as equal as Adam and Eve ... yet they treat us like animals.' Silence. 'And live off our sweat and our strain.'

And now he moves towards us, walking among the crowd.

'The king, together with the lords and bishops, together with the knights and clerks, they arrange it so well! They arrange it so the common people provide their living for them. And how nice it is for them! No wonder they smile at Christmas, when they look at the table spread before them! For we have put it there – though we ourselves starve!

And the common people cannot argue their case, they cannot seek redress, for they do not know their court room Latin ... so theirs is to suffer and theirs is to serve ... and theirs is to hunger night and day!'

No wonder the bishops and Mr Strokelady quibble. No wonder this wandering priest causes a stir. They say the Archbishop of Canterbury will confine him in prison; that he tries to do so now. And I do not remember all his words, just lines here and there. But here is speech I have not met before; words that are inside out in their manner, or upside down.

Mr Ball is not like the friars. He starts not with sin but with poverty. He speaks not of hell in the next life but bondage in this. He speaks as if our bellies are more important than our souls!

And on returning home, (and as secret as I can), I write them down. I copy the words I have heard, as if in the scriptorium. And I write in English, using market words, which somehow seems a sin. I expect my mother up the stairs, or perhaps a priest, standing in the doorway, holding up the cross before my eyes to reprimand me.

'Latin, please! Or face the wrath of God, child!'

But they do not come; I even sleep well, without anxious thoughts. Though as I lie still before sleep, I remember the other strange truth of the day, and the strange truth is this: Sara was there. I am sure I saw Sara in the crowd, listening to John Ball. She wore a shawl and scarf, so I cannot be sure ... yet know that I am.

And I wonder, beneath the harvest moon, what took Sara, my mother's maid, to that field, to listen to such dangerous talk?

*

But as I say, we recover a little, and our bellies also.

The plague took sheep, cows, pigs and chickens - so what have we to sell, when wool and leather are our soul? But there is a season for all things, for dying and for rising, and now animals breed, lambs suck and market stalls begin to re-appear.

Mr Strokelady complains about the city elders' new ordinances. They have appeared after the second visit of the plague, to make the city clean. New laws are made about the disposal of water used in dyeing and tanning. He hates this.

'As if business is not hard enough!'

Neither will animals be allowed to wander so freely through the town, nor their remains lie uncollected. But how can a city ban animals from wandering? How can that work? You might as well ban the wind and the rain.

They believe such laws will keep the plague at bay, perhaps more than our confessions. And maybe they will, I do not know. Such things come too late for me however. They will not bring back Richard and Lettice ... though with each passing year, they are further lost to me, more ghostly.

'Death by ordinance,' says Mr Strokelady, when he hears the new plans. 'If the plague does not kill you, the ordinances will!'

Though he does not get poorer. Indeed, the more he complains, the richer he seems to be. He still has glass in his windows, fresh whitewash on his walls, fine food and wine on his table and fur lining in his coat. Perhaps I should be angry at the rich, like Mr Ball is angry; though I prefer to avoid Mr Strokelady than get angry; and anyway, I hear Mr Ball is now imprisoned. The archbishop has found him; we must hope they treat him kindly.

They will not.

5

And so to the day, the hinge on which the door of my story swings: May 8, in the year of our Lord, 1373. If you wish to know why I am where I am, why the bishop has walled me in and declared me dead, why I deny myself the sky - then you must understand this night, when I was thirty-three years old.

For while I believe everything has led me to this cell - a co-inherence of circumstance - it was my illness, my nearly-death and the visions granted to me at this time which changed all things ... and warmed a cold and hardened soul.

The fever was a May Day arrival, gradual at first. It came as the slow draining of life, as if I wearied a little, then strengthened, until my aching limbs turned to flame ... feelings of burning. I cannot describe the pain and what benefit in such a course?

'I believe I have the plague,' I say to my mother.

'You always believe that, Beatrix.' She believes I invent illness, and sometimes I do, I know ... but not today. 'You smell plague in your bones when you but cough or sneeze! The melancholy will pass.'

'My limbs are aflame, mother. This is no cough ... I feel the sweats.'

I say that I must take me to bed for the afternoon, which she does not like ... but time then collapses, it swirls and it drifts ... long and confused days and nights follow, until I know nothing but pain.

My mother is my nurse, and a good nurse, I believe so, with compresses of yarrow pressed against me; and lemon balm tea held to my lips.

'Drink this if you wish to live, Beatrix.'

I drink and I dribble, I cannot hold it down and relief does not arrive; there is no relief to be found on earth.

And on the fifth night of my suffering, the priest is called.

I had not wished to die, not at the beginning. I had wanted to live, to love God better and for longer on this earth. But I know now my life ebbs away, the pains in my body speak clear; and I accept the will of God with all my heart.

And I say with the Blessed Virgin: 'Let it be to me according to your will.'

So I endure my suffering until day breaks. My body is now without sensation from my waist down, the strangest thing. I desire the sitting pose, with my head leant back, so my heart is better set to God, while yet I am alive.

But my mother believes me dead.

'She is dead,' she says to the priest soon after he arrives. 'My daughter is dead.' And she leans forward to close my eyes, I feel her cool hands. And on hearing the words, and feeling her hands, I truly believe I am so. I believe I am leaving this earth, suffering unto death ... and now death has come, the passing on, the river crossed.

Only I live ... somewhere in my addled frame, I live.

'She is not yet dead,' says the priest.

'She revives?' says my mother.

'She does not revive, no, she weakens; she will not see the morning ... but she breathes, she is not dead.'

And so the priest continues his work. The last rites of Holy Church are bestowed upon me, I remember a little ... an acolyte by his side, a young boy, holding high the cross. The priest reminds me of the Virgin Mary's sweet care for us all ... and now his face coming close to mine for the anointing – fat, sticky fingers on my cold forehead, he asks for confession, but what have I to say? I cannot open my mouth.

He looks at me.

'Do you believe fully that Christ died for you and that you may never be saved but by the merit of Christ's passion?'

'I so believe.'

I speak as if in a dream, but a dark one and with such soreness in my throat. I do not know what is heard.

'In manus tuas commendo spiritum meum,' he says.

I struggle with the bread. The body of Christ is placed on my lips, food for the journey from this life to the next ... but hard and dry, it feels so. His thumb forces it into my mouth, though I cannot swallow and it sticks ... the body of Christ lodged in my mouth.

Now he calls to the boy: 'Thomas, the cross – here!' The boy shuffles in front of me.

'Daughter,' says the priest, 'I have brought you the image of your saviour. Look upon it now, and be comforted in reverence to him who died for you and for me.'

I do not wish to look at the cross, it is not my desire. I wish to look up at heaven where soon I will go. But to look forward is easier than to look up, and so I hold the cross in my sight, and Thomas holds it, his eyes wishing me well ... and all around me becomes dark.

The priest pulls away, I sense him gone. The priest is gone, and I am alone with Thomas and the cross. The priest is washing his hands, cleaning away my contagion.

'Thomas!' he says, and the boy, after a moment's delay, as if to be kind, joins him.

'Hurry yourself, Thomas!' he says. 'She needs the cross no more.'

I see the tall cross lowered through the doorway, they go down the stairs, I hear them; they have done what they can, the last rites performed, and now Holy Church departs. They hand me over, I am left to heaven; or to the land between church and heaven.

I seek guidance. I have not been here before, this netherworld, this small passageway. But I have wished to be here, wished often to leave this earth - though not so enflamed in my joints, and not so meagrely. But I have only to open the door now, the door ahead, the door of heaven, I can see it - surely the door of paradise, an end to the pain, the gateway to eternal life ... will I be met?

I am looking for a door ... but all I see is the cross, now a vision, and it is ugly in my sight, surrounded by fiends who cackle and writhe. And now my upper body joins my lower, it dies to sensation and the greatest pain is my shortness of breath and the failing life within.

I cannot breathe, I have reached the end ... my gasping body spent of life and strength.

But as I gaze on the brutish cross - and I know only the mystery - the most kindly occurrence ... and yet how to speak of it? I do not know how, my words are silly. But I report the entire departure of my pain ... my pain quite gone, eased from me like a donkey relieved of its aching load, all now put down. My pain is gone!

And as sun spills into the room, I feel quite ready to die and eager for it to be so.

'Blessed be the Lord!' I shout and my mother crosses herself, thinking me possessed. But I am not possessed ... for then my visions begin. This is their beginning and for the next five hours - I discover this later - such showings are given to me, such revelations of love! I see them ... but I do not know how I see them.

And afterwards, when I tell my mother what I have seen, she is concerned.

'How did you see?' she asks, in agitation. 'I have not seen such things. They will be from the devil.'

But I do not know how I saw, and I cannot explain; and they are not from the devil, of this I am sure.

'Did you hear voices?'

'I heard Jesus speaking.'

'You will be quiet!'

But I cannot be quiet.

'I heard Jesus speaking.'

'You will not say this!'

I know only that I saw awful and wonderful things, but do not understand. I know only that all things are changed, without knowing how it has occurred. I try to explain.

'My sight began to fail, mother, and it grew dark around me in the room, as dark as night ... except that in the cross there remained a light for all mankind, though I know not how this can be.'

'You can rest now. Calm yourself, child. Be calm and say no more, the priest must not know.'

But I cannot rest, my spirit is bubbling like a stream, like a fountain splintering rocks.

'Everything other than the cross was base to me, mother, and ugly - as if crowded out by fiends of the worst sort. And then with his dear gaze, my Lord led my eyes to his wound - to the wound in his side.'

'I say you must not speak of these things.'

But I do speak.

'And these words, mother, these words were spoken: "You shall not be overcome." They were said distinctly for my assurance and comfort against all the tribulations that may arise.'

'Who said these things?'

'Jesus.'

'Child ...'

'He did not say "You shall not be perturbed" but he did say "You shall not be overcome."' Is that not wonderful? I shall not be overcome!'

Though I lie in my sweat, I wish to run and to laugh, all shame quite gone. I shall not be overcome!

'Really, you must speak of this to no one, and neither will I,' says my mother, as if I have stolen some cloth from the market. Though I do not hear her, or I do not listen; for on waking, pregnant with all I have seen, I lie in a glory other than my own.

And here I pause, covered in sweat ... but within, truly I glow.

*

I sleep awhile, an ecstatic sleep, revisiting scenes from my showings; and then I wake and know that I will live, that I will not die ... not of this illness. My pain is quite gone, I have breath, strong breath. And I remember - lying in the waste and slime of my body - the last words spoken to me by Mother Jesus.

'Know it well,' he said. I hear his words in the room, speaking to me. 'It was no raving you saw today, so take it and believe it. Keep yourself in it, keep yourself in this truth and comfort yourself with it and trust yourself to it. And you will not be overcome.'

I lie awhile, enjoying his words, enjoying the air, enjoying pain's retreat. I notice the roof, the poorly plastered straw and then I call out.

'Mother?'

I hear her on the stairs, she arrives in the doorway.

'So you're awake?'

'I am truly awakened.'

'And not before time.'

'Has the priest gone?'

'He went awhile back and not best pleased,' she says. 'Not pleased at all. He feels himself falsely called.'

'How so?'

'How so, girl? A man offers the last rites and then you live! He might well feel himself a fool. You will need to apologise.'

'I am to apologise for living?' I wonder if it is my mother who feels a fool and attacks me for that. 'I did not call him, mother. I believe you called him.'

'As I do everything - though not for thanks it seems! Would there was someone to look after me! You lie there for days ...'

'I am mended,' I say, 'quite mended. Thank you for the lemon balm.'

There is a pause.

'It always worked for your father, I did my best, until – well, nothing heals the judgement of the plague.'

'No.'

'Sinners should not expect fortune.'

My heart sinks. She speaks as Mother Church; they speak in the same manner. They use these words, 'no fortune for sinners', though such words do not appeal to me now. I let them be, I do not argue. But they do not ring true in my heart ... they ring like a broken bell. Richard and Lettice saw no fortune, their plagued bodies drained of blood and moisture, dry and pale, ashen and exhausted, turning the colour of blue ...and the church says they sinned, though I saw no sin at all.

No sin ...

*

Yet I now live. I breathe in life and I delight in my living. I have visited death, I have walked its tunnel and knocked at its door ... but returned. I survive both plague and illness, and as I lie here, I take sweet pleasure in my settled breath ... and know peace beyond words. In my heart, I run with joy like, once, I ran with Richard before we wed. We ran together laughing, imagining all would be well, as young people dare to believe.

'And sadly chamber pots don't empty themselves,' says my mother, still in the doorway. She has never liked me still. 'Just as well we aren't all ill.'

'Do not be anxious,' I say to her, raising myself on my elbow and turning towards her. I am surprised to hear myself speak in this way, most surprised; I have not heard these words from my mouth before. 'You shall not be overcome, mother.'

'I don't know what you talk of,' she says, looking sad for a moment; and then she leaves me with my happy wounds. 'And we'll need fresh straw for your mattress,' she calls from the stairs. 'You can't lie in that, it's not right. So when you're recovered - and you look recovered to me - you'll need to pack fresh straw.'

And I know - somewhere within I know - that I must hide in some manner; I know this straight away. I will need to hide. And over the coming days, I understand more fully, as the meaning of these showings becomes plainer in my sight. I know in my heart I must withdraw with these visions. I will protect them, like one who guards a weak flame in the wind.

And I come to this awareness, with assurance, in the home of Mr Aske. He bakes for our street in the Conisford area of Norwich. I have come to buy a loaf and stand in the kitchen where the large oven door is ajar. I enjoy its charming heat on my body, but upon realising, Mr Aske moves quickly to close it.

'Nothing bakes with the oven door open!' he says cheerfully.

'No,' I reply, sad to lose the warmth.

'Open the oven door and the heat is gone, Beatrix - quite lost and no rising within.'

The thought of such loss scares me ... and all is clear. I do not wish to lose my visions, and so decide to write them down, if this is possible. (It might be like trying to catch the wind.) But where and how might I do this, when neither my mother nor the priests will allow?

I remember Sister Rachel, the anchoress, and know I too must withdraw. I seem to know this. I know I must withdraw both to ponder and write freely of these things. It will be for no one but myself; I shall not share this work and thereby trouble the church. I do not wish to trouble Mother Church. And I will write nothing that is contrary to her teaching.

But I must withdraw, I must close the oven door, to hold in the heat and allow this divine dough to rise in my soul, with no one watching on.

'It is good to see you here,' says Mr Aske. 'We thought we'd lost you, Beatrix.'

'I thought myself lost as well.'

'I heard the priest came.'

'He came kindly, but was not needed.'

'Your mother thought you dead?' He says it with a smile. I sense he does not like her.

'And I thought myself so. But I recover well, thank you.'

'Gave you the last rites, I hear?'

He packs loaves together on a large wooden tray as he speaks.

'We are all mistaken sometimes, Mr Aske.'

'Quite, quite. Though you still look weak to me, you poor girl. Mrs Aske and I, we did pray.'

'Then your prayers were answered, praise God.'

'But you must go careful now. Or who will look after your mother in her old age?'

'Indeed.'

And then at the door, he stops me, with a gift. 'Here, take an extra bun for strength.'

*

I make my way home, and trip slightly and stumble ... I am still weak. But I do not wish for the pity of Mr Aske or any other; and neither do I deserve it. For I had asked for this illness. It is best I make it known. When young, I asked for just such an illness as this.

Does this surprise you? That a child should ask for such a thing? That a child should demand pain? It is, however, quite true; I do not lie. Though had I known what pain it would bring, I would have been loathe to pray for it.

But when young, with a young heart, I had demanded this suffering of God and was most firm in my asking, as one desperate and sure. I did not know what I asked, I knew nothing. How can a child know what they ask? Yet I had asked nonetheless.

My small self was determined to suffer. Little Beatrix wished to be taken to the edge of life, to the utmost brink, to be held over the yawning abyss, to feel the terror and spiritual pains. And why? So I might know Christ's own suffering, and the suffering of his mother Mary, and live more wholly for God's honour thereafter.

And perhaps be free of shame? I move fast from bliss to self-disgust, I know this is so; I move between the two. In moments of joy, I might say with St Paul 'Nothing can separate me from the love of Christ.' And in the moments of sorrow, I might scream with St Peter, 'Lord save me, for I perish!'

I never told my mother of these demands. She would not understand and would not view the matter with kindness. She would ask me why I gave her such worry; and I would not know what to say.

But I still desired illness unto death. And I wished to be St Cecilia. This is the heart of the matter. I wished to be St Cecilia.

*

I remember the day the friar told us her story; and St. Cecelia, the bravest of the brave, never left me thereafter, not for one day. I demanded that her path be my path; and her path was both suffering and light.

As a girl, I was dutiful. I tried to please ... to please all. This is right, is it not? And first of all, one must please one's parents. But in some manner, I craved more than those around me. Who knows where or when such desire was sown in me? But I looked beyond my parents. And desired something more demanding than mere daily prayer and the mass, so easily performed, and so promptly forgot.

Some wish for religious ease, I know this; but I did not wish for ease ... I desired more for my restless heart and mind. I desired for myself the very mind of Christ, union with God beyond mere religious duty.

I could feel the Passion of Christ strongly – how could I not? Yet I longed, by God's grace, to feel it more intensely still. I wanted to stand with our Lord's suffering and our Lady's suffering ... to suffer with them. And to this sweet end, I desired a bodily sickness that would lead me to death; at least to death's door, this was my prayer.

And I wished for the three wounds of St Cecelia.

She was a girl in ancient Rome whose pagan family demanded she marry, as daughters must ... we are all told to marry, or re-marry, even before our husband's body is cold. But Cecelia did not wish for this yoking and refused her parents. She said she would not walk their path or fit herself into their desires. She told them God called her to celibacy ... to an adventure other than their choosing.

Her family ignored her request; her desires were regarded as nothing. They imagined a foolish head on their young daughter and married her to the man of their choosing, an unbeliever.

But on her wedding night – and here is the wonder - instead of bodily union, she converted her husband to the Christian way and preserved also her virginity. The two of them then converted their friends and families to Jesus; and in fury at their deeds, the Roman authorities killed Cecelia's husband and arrested her.

She was taken to the Roman provost. Standing before him, he asked her:

'Do you know what power I possess?'

'Your power is little to dread,' she replied, 'for it is like a bladder full of wind, which, with the prick of a needle, is gone and is nothing anymore.'

The enraged provost, his neck a-sweat, ordered Cecelia's death. But when the soldiers tried to cut off her head, they found themselves thwarted by the power of God. Three times they struck at her neck with an axe, the most strikes allowed by their law. But they did not kill her. She lived on for three days with her wounds, healing and saving many.

'So let *my* wounds heal many!' This was the desire of Little Beatrix.

6

'**M**r Curtgate tells me you want to hide away, girl! Is the world too grievous for you – or too rough?!'

These are Bishop Henry's greeting words. He declares from behind a large table in the hall of the Bishop's Palace. The grand hall is bigger than any room I have seen; it is the size of the market place. And he is surrounded by robes, with men inside - clergy and lawyers, I imagine, each with a task and a bow ... but I notice only Bishop Henry. He stands before me, hands on hips, in his clean-shaven, red-faced ebullience, lord of all he surveys ... he surveys me intensely.

'Not too grievous, my Lord Bishop,' I reply. 'I find it too full of God to be grievous.' The bishop raises his eyebrows. 'But our Lord has different callings for his children, this I have come to see. We cannot all be as you, though we might wish it.'

Bishop Henry laughs, sits down and puts his head in his hands. It is quite plain from his manner that I stand before episcopal incomprehension.

'But to be walled in, woman? Do you really wish to be walled in like a prisoner, kennelled like a dog? Do you wish to be a captive, with nothing but a window and a bed of straw? Our prisons are full of such folk - and they wish to be elsewhere!' The robed hall laughs. 'Is this really your wish for your life, to be so alone?'

'My Lord, I do not expect you to join me there.'

There is silence. The robes in the room are anxious. They wonder if these words of mine are well-considered. I sense their unease and believe the bishop himself wonders the same, being mindful of his position. And then he breaks out into loud laughter and finds quick company for his mirth, the acolytes grinning at this odd woman - this is their thought; though the hunched Roger Curtgate, priest of St Julian's, looks ill.

And I am grateful to this kindly man. It is Mr Curtgate who has brought me here and arranged this meeting. It was he who fitted this awkward and un-fitting soul into the bishop's hurried day. But then I was also a determined woman in the matter - determined behind my cause, which proved necessary. For when I spoke of my desire to withdraw from the world, some suggested I be a nun.

'You would be a good nun,' they said, as though they spoke for the angels. 'And you help out in the kitchens at Carrow Abbey, do you not?'

'I do sometimes.'

'Then you are made for that - being a widow; you should quite definitely be a nun.'

But that was not my sense. I had seen the nuns at Carrow Abbey and felt it too crowded a way, too closely peopled. And what if the other nuns did not help me? People do not always help each other. There is jealousy and malice behind holy walls as well as kindness, which can make for misery. I was drawn by the power of alone; I felt this ... the call to learn the friendship of solitude. So I said I would not be a nun.

'There will be much scrutiny,' says Mr Curtgate when we speak of withdrawal. 'Your calling will need testing by Mother Church.'

'I do not need it tested,' I reply. 'I know it to be true.'

I hold Mother Church in high regard, and yield to her in all things, as a simple child must. But I do not need her opinion in this circumstance. I need only her blessing.

'But the bishop must know the same,' says Mr Curtgate. 'He must know your calling to be true.'

'And how will he know?' I ask for I cannot see how he will know. 'Shall I tell him?'

Mr Curtgate snorts in anxious laughter.

'I don't believe you should tell him.'

'Then again I ask: how will he know?'

'He will know because -' and here Mr Curtgate falters a little. ' – because he is your father in God.'

And Lord forgive me, but I bridle at this.

'You said he was a soldier; that he likes to talk of old wars, of the glory of Crecy.'

'A soldier he is, and a brave one, Beatrix, there is no question of that.' He seems eager to reassure me. 'He has campaigned in England, Scotland, France and Flanders. We are certainly safer for his presence among us.'

'For myself, I do not feel safer,' I say, 'for I did not feel unsafe before, Mr Curtgate. I do not need another to feel safe.'

'Perhaps another can at least help us feel safe.'

Mr Curtgate does not look as one who feels at all safe; though God wishes safety for us all.

'I merely wish to be an anchoress,' I say. 'This is my calling; and you have kindly offered your church for my anchorhold. So you trust my calling, I presume this?'

I speak plainly to him.

'I do trust your calling, Beatrix.'

'Julian. I shall be called Julian.'

'Julian?'

'Julian, yes. I shall call myself by the church's name.'

'Then yes, Julian - I trust your feelings to be sincere.'

'And that is not quite the same.'

'Well, it is my present knowing. How can I know anything else?'

'And your knowing, so-called, will support me before the bishop?'

'I will support you, as long as ...'

'As long as what?'

'As long as my Lord Bishop supports you.'

'Then you do not support me.'

'I can present you before him, as a seeker; but I can hardly support you before he has heard your case.'

'My case? Is this a trial in law as though I am a thief?'

'Your sense needs a trial. There can be no entitlement in this matter, only a testing of the spirits.'

I do not know what to do with my fury, but find myself smiling. I have always worn a smile over my rage, wishing to deflect.

'I seek a cell built on the side of St Julian's. I seek to be an anchoress - one anchored, with stability of place. I seek a life of contemplation and prayer. It is my calling. What case is there that needs such testing?'

'It is for life.'

'It is for life, yes. That does not appear to me as threat.'

'Well, you say that now, Beatrix ...'

'Julian.'

'Julian, yes ... you say that now beneath the sun and the sky. But you will not have the sun and the sky where you go, neither the moon nor the stars. Nor a husband's touch.' I believe he blushes a little. 'You must be as sure in your heart in this matter. It is like entering a marriage, there can be no doubts.'

'I was not sure about my marriage, Mr Curtgate.' I have to tell him this. 'Do I surprise you?'

'Well ...'

'How can one be sure of the future? Or sure of another? One might grow into the marriage, one might not. But how can one know certainty at the beginning?'

This was my way, my marriage needed to grow, though I do not believe he has pondered the matter, and he changes course. 'I heard of an anchoress who went quite mad, throwing herself against the walls of her cell unto death.'

And so he does not answer my question, but tells me instead another unfortunate anchoress story ... there seems to be a well of them, each one eagerly drawn to the surface for my benefit.

'No one could help her,' he adds. 'And it was not permitted for them to enter ... nor for her to leave.'

'I shall ask for the help of God,' I say, knowing this to be quite sufficient and bored of this talk.

'I believe she did the same.'

'I cannot speak for her.'

'But you can take notice. The bishop called her a fool.'

'I am surprised he had time between battles.'

'I hardly think ...'

'And I suppose you see me in the same light, Mr Curtgate?' I suddenly see this. 'Do you call me a fool as well? Or perhaps think it privately?'

'There is loneliness and desolation in withdrawal; it is not unknown.'

'Maybe for some.'

'And some withdraw because they cannot get along with other souls and prove friendless in the street. We must know our reasons for our acts, however virtuous they may appear.'

'And you believe that to be me?'

'No, no – I merely say that I see no Christian benefit in this cell.'

'No benefit?'

'We are called to love our neighbour, not turn our back on him ... or our families.' There is silence between us before he speaks again; though he does not look at me. 'And your mother is not pleased,' he adds and my eyebrows rise.

'My mother? She has spoken with you?'

'She has had words with me.'

'She has no word in this matter.'

'I believe she has.'

'And I believe she does not, Mr Curtgate; God's call does not come through our parents.'

'I merely say ...'

'Then you do not say well.'

'We must honour our mothers, I believe.' I stand in silence. I have no need to add to his discomfort. 'I believe so. And the bishop will need to be reassured as to payment.'

'Payment?'

'This calling must be paid for, Beatrix.'

'Julian.'

'Julian, yes. It must be paid for.'

'I do not understand.'

'Well, he will not do it himself.'

'I believe my soul to be the bishop's responsibility.'

'You are his responsibility – by church law,' he says, nodding.

'And I believe he has enough coins.'

'These are hard times, Julian. Poverty abounds.'

'It does not abound in his palace, Mr Curtgate ... I have not heard stories of lack in that place ... rather the opposite.' Mr Curtgate's discomfort, displayed in his shifting eyes, fills the room. But I am not done. 'I am part of the church, part of the body of Christ, surely?'

'You are indeed, Beatrix.'

'Julian.'

'Julian, yes. But you are not a body part His Lordship will fund; his chaplain has made this clear to me. Very clear. His Grace has other demands on his coffers.'

'He has demands other than the perpetual prayer of an anchoress for this city?'

I do not feel I have ever been so angered as I am in this moment.

'Mother Church never sleeps in these troubled times.'

'They have been troubled since Eden.'

'Quite, quite. But the Pope demands constant payment, a great drain on English funds ...a very great drain.'

'The Pope is now our enemy?'

'I do not say that, I do not say that ... no, not at all.' Mr Curtgate's head is shaking, furious with denial. I believe he finds problem in my resolve, though he now attempts to calm. He whips up a storm ... and then begs the wind to drop! 'But the good people of the parish promise support,' he says. 'This is the good news, Beatrix.'

'Julian.'

'Julian, yes. *Julian.* I know you now desire a new name. But I have known you a long time by the other. And you are not yet an anchoress.'

'I am in my heart ... I already am.'

'Your heart does not decide the issue; the bishop will do that. But as I say, the parishioners promise food at least - and perhaps candles.'

'Then I have food and light!'

'And we will hope for some bequests. I have heard anchorites receive generous bequests in return for their prayers. The dying can be generous.'

'If frightened enough of purgatory,' I say, and not with warmth. 'I do not wish to collect money from people's fear.'

'And your servant will need paying.'

'Sara has agreed to support me, with or without payment.'

'It is better with payment.'

'She cares not.'

'Especially in a January wind, when the earth is hard and the chamber pot full. On those days, it is good to know you are paid for your troubles.'

He clearly does not know Sara and I cannot imagine a polite answer; grace must sometimes stay quiet ... and so it was that we arrived at the bishop's palace. Mr Curtgate stands now in the shadows behind me.

'And you have not considered the married way?' continues the bishop. He still tries to make sense of these affairs.

'Marriage was a most happy state. But it was taken from me, my Lord, by the plague ... both my husband and my child. '

'Then take it back!' he says. 'Take it back! A comely girl like yourself? And there are more children inside you, I'll wager! I see how the men here gaze on you, like kingfishers eyeing trout. And we must re-stock our city, do you not think? I would have you myself!'

'I would not be worthy, your Grace. I am an unlettered soul who seeks only to pray.'

'How old are you?'

'Thirty-three, my Lord.'

'You imagine yourself past such adventures, your juices drying?'

'We must weave with the wool we are given, my Lord. The farmer can work harder than hard – but he cannot change the weather.'

'And what is that supposed to mean?'

'In the end, whatever our plans, my Lord Bishop, there is only trust; trust that all shall be well. This, I believe, is our calling ... deep trust.'

I sense the bishop tiring of my company.

'I have no barrier to put in this maid's way,' he says, bringing our meeting to an end ... or so I believe. 'No barrier between herself and her cell. I mean, do you have any barriers, Curtgate?'

I hope he does not mention my mother.

'If my Lord Bishop is happy ...'

'You are allowed a view, man!' Mr Curtgate nods, though he does not offer a view and the bishop gives up his baiting. 'And I hear you have support in place, is that so?'

'It is so,' I say.

'Support from your parishioners, Curtgate?' He nods again, unable to speak. 'Everyone must eat, after all –even an anchoress! And get the bequests coming in, that's the trick, sister - get those bequests falling into your lap. Prayer should most definitely be paid for, and no one likes the idea of purgatory, damnable place - we all want quick passage through there, and we'll pay any amount for prayers that make it more brief.' There is sudden unease in the bishop's face. 'Not that

I want you taking any money destined for the church, you understand - we need every blessed groat!' Mr Curtgate is again nodding in agreement, as if we listen to the beatitudes.

'My husband's family,' I say, 'have also made some provision, my Lord ... in their kindness.'

'Well, that may help you until Christmas - but beyond that, it is the bequests trade for you, sister; and then you'll be fine - they'll keep you in eggs, fish and beer. And you can pray for my soul as well.'

'I shall pray for it daily, my Lord. And thank you.'

He pauses and again looks me in the eye.

'Not a friend of Wyclif, are you?'

'Who?'

I have not heard this name.

'The Oxford bastard – John Wyclif.'

Now Mr Curtgate looks worried; I seem to note his reactions more than my own. He is a weather vane for me, a teller of approaching church storms which I do not see coming.

'I do not believe so, my Lord. I do not know any man called Wyclif.'

I speak the name carefully to make sure I have heard the bishop aright. Our neighbour is called Mr.Wickiffe and I do not wish later to discover the bishop has referred to him. I know Mr Wickiffe well; and have always known him as a reasonable man.

'A great writer of tracts, Wyclif, hiding away in Oxford ... tracts in English and tracts full of shit. He stirs people against the Pope, against mother church ... fit for the sewer that one, a pig-faced prick louse, but protected by John of fucking Gaunt ... and protected by the fucking university.'

This is not our neighbour, unless I mis-read him badly.

'He wouldn't survive in Norwich, he'd be a dead man, noosed and slit ... no protectors here for him or his blabbering horse-shit-eating Lollardy friends ... but you don't know him, you say.'

'I do not know him, my Lord.'

'Then may Christian charity speed you on your way, woman!' He is now striding towards the door, though he looks round once, to say: 'You shall be an anchoress, if that is your wish!'

'It is my wish.'

'Then pray for this great city of ours until your knees are sore! We bloody well need it!'

And there I pause, allowing the memory to fade, returning to the stillness of my cell; for the bishop is not still.

*

'Who is this Wyclif gentleman?' I ask Mr Curtgate as we walk away from the palace and towards St Julian's.

We return to his church, whose name I have taken. I now call myself Julian in preparation; I leave Beatrix behind, and with little sadness ... though it is further reason for my mother's displeasure. She says this is poor payment for the care she has given me. She says I cast aside my family, though I would call it a behovely thing ... like the shell of a nut falling away, when its use is done.

My mother says she will always call me Beatrix.

'You do not wish to know of Mr Wyclif,' says Mr Curtgate. 'Really, you do not.'

Mr Curtgate seems glad to be standing in the church graveyard, where my cell will be built and where I will spend the rest of my life; I think of this, for a moment. I feel a terror, it passes through and leaves ... but I wish my question answered: who is Mr Wyclif?

'I would not have asked, if I did not wish to know.'

Why would I pose a question if I do not wish to know the answer?

'He is not a friend of the bishop's.'

'I gathered as much.' I cannot help but laugh a little. 'But is he a friend of yours?'

'A friend of mine? Why do you say that?' His hands come together in awkwardness, as if they writhe, like snakes in a fire. 'And I believe you may call me Roger,' he says, 'it would not be unseemly. We are to live close, in a manner.'

But I cannot call him Roger; I know I cannot.

'I shall call you Mr Curtgate for now; it is perhaps more seemly.' I prefer 'Mr Curtgate' - and a name is just a name; I mean no offence, though I feel it taken. 'And Mr Wyclif?' I ask again.

'It will be simpler for you to remain unacquainted with his teaching.'

'How can I judge?'

'A clever man, there is no doubt about that ... most clever.'

'Clever with what?'

I do not give up and he gives in.

'He causes trouble for the church, and does it often. He is clever.'

'So you say.'

'But a disturber of the peace, our Mr Wyclif.' He looks around to make sure his words are not heard; but only the dead listen to our converse.

'I believe our Lord also caused trouble,' I remind him.

'Well, that may be so, but ... '

'So what does he do - this terrible man? I confess a distrust of other people's opinions. I struggle to trust them ... it is a gaping sin of mine.'

'He attacks everything and everyone from his hideaway in Balliol College in Oxford.'

'Oxford?'

'There is a university there. It is a place of learning.'

'They have books?'

'They have a great many books.' It sounds wonderful. 'But it is small ... not like Norwich. And whether they truly learn there ...'

'My place of learning was an illness and a bed,' I say firmly. 'I needed no books ... so Oxford can keep them!' I do not quite mean this. I would like them to send me some.

'And from there, he attacks – Wyclif attacks, well, many practices.'

'What sort of practices?'

'He opposes pilgrimages undertaken to worship the holy relics. He does not like those.'

'Why?'

'He does not believe the relics to be holy.'

'I see.'

I am somewhere between shock and laughter.

'He does not believe it is truly wood from the cross of Christ or the thorns from his crown or the leather from his sandals. He believes such things to be fakery, created to fill the church coffers.'

'I do hear our Lord's sandals must have been the size of a large boat, and that his cross would stretch from here to Yarmouth.'Again, Mr Curtgate looks round.

'Do not jest – please, do not.'

'So do you believe them to be true, Mr Curtgate?'

'Do I believe what to be true?'

'The relics.'

'Me – well ... as Pilate said, 'What is truth?''

'I believe a vicar should know it; or what hope for us normal Christians?'

'Relics can be a great support to people.'

'But do you believe in your soul that these things are true to what they claim? Leather from his actual sandals?'

'What does it matter what I believe to be true in my soul?'

He shakes his head.

'It matters a great deal, Mr Curtgate, for the soul is in the middle of the heart.'

'You are my teacher now?'

'I am no one's teacher, not even my own; but I have seen this to be so, the Lord opened my eyes in a vision.'

'Visions are not scripture.'

'And I saw that Jesus resides in our soul, in peace and in rest. He resides there. We cannot therefore place a lie in our soul, to sit alongside him. How could we place a lie alongside our Lord?'

He looks at me with concern. He opens the church door and we step into the dark, away from the world. The immediate quiet of the sanctuary can be touched; the stillness is delicious to my senses ... though Mr Curtgate needs to speak again. He has much to say about Mr Wyclif; and I begin to regret my question, for this holy space is kinder without words ... it is more holy in quiet.

'He doesn't like clergy too busy counting money to attend services.'

'Do any of us applaud such folk?' I ask.

'And I don't say it doesn't happen, it happens too much, I know it happens; and all that Mr Wyclif says is true - all of it.'

'All of it?'

'But really, well – there must be respect. And rules. I think there should be respect and rules.' We sit and gaze at the crucifix on the altar. I have joined him in the pew. 'Mr Wyclif says all the church's troubles arise from men seeking money and power,' he adds.

Mr Curtgate is tired, his skin pale. I do believe the visit to the bishop has quite exhausted him.

'And then, of course, he says it all goes to Rome.'

'What goes to Rome?'

'The English money, it drains away to Rome, like a leak in a tub.' He again uses the word 'drains'. 'The Pope takes five times more than the English king!' he says. 'And for what reason, and for what good, this endless draining?'

'The Pope is our father in God.'

This is my understanding, and the words I am taught.

'Wyclif says there is more purity in a whore,' he says and truly, I am shocked to hear this in his mouth ... and in a church. 'We have two Popes, one in Rome, one in Avignon – and they excommunicate each other!' I find myself puzzled; it seems I know little of Mother Church. 'I'm not on Wyclif's side, sister!' he adds hastily. 'You must never say I am on his side, not to any person. Are you on his side? You must keep quiet if you are!'

'I don't believe our courteous Lord has sides. He is for us all.'

'Mr Wyclif calls the faith of monks 'a religion of fat cows.'

'I have met some well-girthed friars ...'

'But does he speak wisely? That is the question. Perhaps people like him should be more discreet; be less busy in speaking. We are not all as well protected as he; and there will only be trouble. '

'Trouble?'

'I mean, the Lollardy fellows. There will be trouble for them.'

I long again for quiet in God's house. Does he imagine salvation comes through wordery? But my questions feed the fire and I have another now.

'Who are they, these Lollards? I do hear the word shouted.'

I do not wish to ask; I do not wish to know. The world's talk dulls my flame, dousing it, enfeebling my spirit. I wish to be alone with my Lord. And yet questions flood my mind.

'Those who follow Wyclif, they are called "Lollards",' he says. 'You must know them, they're everywhere.'

'My Lord Bishop spits the word - as though it is excrement in his mouth.'

'They're here, you know - here among us.' He speaks in a whisper; he speaks as if they carry the plague, as if they steal milk from the children, and then batter their heads. 'They say that if you see five men talking in Norwich, three of them are Lollards.'

'Is that so? Then I must know the other two,' I say, to calm his agitation. I do not know any Lollards ... or I do not believe I do ... and do not care if I do or I don't.

'They say the Pope jokes about the English. They say he takes us for fools. "The English are good asses," he says in his palace. "For they carry well all the loads I lay on them!"

'I have no interest in the Pope, Mr Curtgate ... just my cell.'

Another silence follows. Mr Curtgate appears conflicted in his mind.

'The building starts tomorrow,' he says. 'God willing.'

'The building of the cell?'

He nods and is suddenly standing, moving towards the north side of the church. 'I have been promised that it starts tomorrow. And this here will be your window into the nave.'

'My Christ window. It will be a holy vista.'

'Quite. Though I am sad, of course, that you will not be able to join us.'

'Join you?'

'Some anchorites use the church as well as the cell, as I have mentioned to you.'

'Yes.'

'They have a door through to the church, which they may visit and use as they wish. It could be good for you. You did say you would reflect on this.'

'It was a kind suggestion, Mr Curtgate; and I have reflected on it.'

'You have?'

'And while it remains kind, I believe a simple cell, without exit, is my calling.'

We had spoken of this yesterday and he had not taken my feelings well. I offered to reflect on the matter to please him; but not to change my mind.

'You prefer a wall between us?'

'It will not be a wall to me, Mr Curtgate; just the shape of my being ... as our clothing both shapes us towards others and separates.' This had been the picture which came to me. 'I do not see your robe as a wall between us and nor will I see these stones in that manner.'

I do not know how Mr Curtgate receives this, but I speak the words sincerely. I know also that if I have a door into the church, then they have a door into the cell, which does not attract me. I need safety unto death and control of my home.

'The master builder will construct a support across here.' He shows me the place where my cell will join the church. 'A stone arch, he said. And with the bishop's permission now granted, they can start work tomorrow.'

'Well, that is timely.'

I confess impatience; I have found the journey slow.

'It may not be tomorrow.'

'But he said it would be tomorrow.'

I see no reason to delay.

'He said tomorrow, yes; but, Mr Mason – what he says and does, well ...'

Again, the priest looks haunted.

'Are you happy of spirit, Mr Curtgate?'

'Happy of spirit?'

'You seem perturbed.'

'I am not perturbed.'

He is perturbed.

'And though it is not my place, for I am but a poor unlettered woman - I would wish you at peace.'

'Who is not perturbed on occasion, Beatrix?'

'Julian.'

'Julian, yes.'

'Are you perhaps perturbed about me?'

'You did not mention your visions to the bishop.'

'He did not ask after them. And you did counsel a quiet tongue on the matter.'

'Quite, quite.'

I am confused. I do not know why Mr Curtgate has agreed to host my cell beside his church. He seems a troubled man ... and I am yet more trouble. His shoulders are bent beneath the weight of his worries. Though some need must drive his cautious soul ... some wish must sit there, some desire; for truly, to say 'no' to my cause would have been the easier way.

'Do you still wish me here, Mr Curtgate?'

'Of course, I ...'

'You must not do what you do not wish to do.'

'I do not ...'

'You married Richard and I in this place, a most joyful day; and you buried Richard and Lettice outside, a sad day. We have journeyed together, Mr Curtgate, I know this. But these are not reasons to say 'Yes."

'I want you here ... Julian. We need say no more.'

'Are you sure? I will be trouble, I am sure.'

'I want you here. And pray for me.'

And there I pause. I do not know why he wishes me here.

7

It is my final night before I enter the cell. Tomorrow, I will be buried. Our house is quiet, the candles are stilled; and beyond, my plagued city sleeps ... so many dead, and so many gone, the ghosts outnumber the living.

These many homes, so many homes, and restless tonight in the marshland sulk with the dreams and nightmares that spill out of sleep; I know them well ... and always the tannery stench. But I do not wish to leave this place; that is not my desire. An anchoress, like a tree, is rooted; and I wish to be rooted here.

'I am not leaving Norwich!' I have said this to Sara, who speaks as if I depart for a faraway land.

'Make more sense if you did,' she replies to me. 'Too much of the big city for me here. I'm just a girl from Essex - Kelvedon born and bred - who can't abide the stink.'

'But big cities must stink, Sara!' I tell her this. 'They are big because they work, and work stinks - especially the fisheries and the tanning.' Perhaps only a city girl understands this.

I will take my last walk beneath the stars. And while I dearly love these people, I will miss the stars the more. My head covered, I step out into the night air.

'Lollard bastard!'

There is shouting on the street ahead. They stagger and lurch with beer and become loose with their mouths and fists. Everyone is named a Lollard these days, when out of favour and when tempers and hatred are stirred.

Something is thrown, I hear it; pottery smashes and breaks, there is laughter, then a grunt. I withdraw into the shadows, but I think they fight and the night watchman arrives.

'Who goes there?' he shouts in the darkness, 'Declare yourselves!'

There is no reply; and after some while, the watchman leaves; and again I proceed beneath the sky, along Glovers Street with its shuttered windows, the silence settling again. It does arrive, even in a city so busy by day; and this is a busy city, especially harbour-side, where I will dwell. St Julian's is near the harbour - and my cell, harbour-side, where I've always felt at home.

And I remember my father ... I remember him boasting.

'We send back better goods than we receive, girl ... honest English goods. Fine wool from our sheep, the best sheep, no one has our sheep ... nor our soft leather, our wholesome wheat, or our stained glass – 'stained by angels" he said 'and such carved wood! No finer carpenters than Norwich carpenters.'

He would have liked Richard, had he been allowed to live; had they both been allowed to live ... though he laughed at my love of stories.

'Fancy imaginings do not cook a turnip,' he would say when I spoke of my desire to write. 'How can a woman write? And what shall she write about? Better a clean piece of leather or a loaf of spiced bread.'

It is not useful, I know this. Writing is not useful and my mother likes me useful, as she is useful. She must always be useful, always be doing something. She never sits quiet in our cobbled street, which is better than those of mud. Those are the poorer sorts, streets of mud, and we are not poor, my mother says this; our street is cobbled. And while we have only stools and benches, some homes in our road have chairs. Mr Strokelady has eight chairs, I counted them.

And maybe my father would be against me now; I admit this for a moment ... we do make saints of the dead, and make them for our purposes. But these thoughts melt as I walk beneath the big sky, for my heart is the stronger voice; and I cannot fight what people think of what I do ... but simply walk the path given. And as I walk, I say goodbye; I find this sense arising in me, a strange emptying of all that has been.

'For all that has been, thank you,' I say. 'And for all that shall be, yes!'

And standing at the harbour's edge, the water dark and cold, I throw three sticks into the flow, each with a kiss for their journey. Richard. Lettice ... and myself. They must make their different ways; and I must travel on without them.

'What are you doing here, young lady?'

I look up, fearful. A watchman is standing across the track, the moon lights him well. He is concerned, he seeks to help, I suppose; though he intrudes and I do not wish him here.

'Seeking solitude with the harbour sky,' I say. 'For tomorrow, I die.'

8

It is the day of my walling in, and the hour.

The bishop declares funeral words outside; but I am now enclosed, a body in a tomb; with choice, though without. I can do no other.

I could walk free from this containment. I could push the wall down, the clay is soft. I could push it down now and walk from this place. I think this, as I move away from Sara's window and feel the dark of the cell. I will get used to the dark. I cannot burn candles all day, there are not the funds. So I must become its familiar, make light and dark as one, this will become so.

It is cold, though, and I feel the chill as the words are spoken beneath the March sky, ashes to ashes, dust to dust, for this is my death. I will not leave this place; I make a vow for life, there is no return.

And the bishop has not been unkind. He calls me misguided, 'like a girl lost in a wood' ... but not a heretic. He cannot understand such withdrawal, such separation from the world, this flight from child-bearing and wifely pleasures - he is more soldier than priest, happier in battle than prayer. And what battles can there be in a cell?

'The sword is the best prayer,' he says. 'And fire.'

He is most happy with a warrior God - this I can see, a God as angry as himself. But this is not a God I know, not in any manner; though who I do know, the nature of our sweet Lord, I am still discovering since the showings.

I have not spoken of these to anyone; nor do I know what meaning to find in them. This is why I am here, with my heart and my pen. I shall find their meaning; or their meaning will find me. They are like dry tinder within my soul waiting for the spark; then I imagine they will burn.

But let me write this, and write it early, even as my prison walls dry: they do not make me good. These visions I received, they do not make me better than others; and if I speak of them, it is not as one stuffed with pride, this would be a long cart ride from the truth. I am not good because of these visions ... unless also I love God better.

This is my point. There are many who have received no vision, and yet they love God better than me. I loved my child, and perhaps my husband; but whether I love God ...

'You do truly want this, mistress?' says Sara, through the window. She will look after me in my death. She appears at the window, away from the bishop and the chanting robes around him. 'I only ask.'

Sara makes me smile with her checking, though her words bring fear, like an ill breeze - a doubtful fear, which has neither value nor truth, for I have chosen this way with care.

'You do truly want this, mistress?'

Of course I want it. I say this to myself and know it in my mind. Yet there is always the wondering, 'Have I chosen aright?'

Sister Lucy had said: 'You cannot know if you want it, until it is too late to change your mind.'

And now time runs fast against a change of heart; with the stones put in place, one by one. I am plastered in and closed in, the bricks filling the door through which I have been led, through which I have entered, saying goodbye to the sky ... my door becoming a wall.

'I believe so,' I reply to Sara. 'As long as you will look after me.'

'I will look after you, mistress, this we have agreed. But you say goodbye to the sky and I know you like the sky, the sun and the moon.'

'I will still see the sky.' The chimney allows me a glimpse. 'My eyes will follow the smoke to the heavens.'

'It will be the patch on an apron and no more.'

'I only need a patch. The sky, the sun, the moon and stars, they are in my soul. Now, please ...'

'I have said this before, I know, mistress ... but I worry.'

'Then don't worry, Sara. And I am not your mistress ... and the bishop is talking!'

The funeral liturgy is drawing to a close. The incense wafts, scented smoke, the scent of myrrh, beautiful and sad.

'There's no evil in walking free, mistress.'

'To be as free as you?' I jest and I do not jest. 'Who around you is free, Sara, look about you! Do you see any who are free? Remember, I know these people.'

'We are not caged as you.'

'There are different cages and various entrapments. Is my mother free?'

'We will not speak now of your mother.'

'I am sorry.'

I have no wish to be sharp, but my patience is holed, and Sara - does she know what it is to be free? Has she ever been free in her thirty-five years? Held together by her worries and her work ... yet kind to me, I know not why.

'I'm sure the good bishop won't take offence,' says Sara. 'He will hardly cry at a change of mind. He does not know tears.'

'The bishop would be much grieved, you know this. He would never again believe a woman.'

'He can only roar a little.'

'He roars loudly.'

'And then you would be free.'

'I am free,' I say in the darkness.

And Sara turns away from my words, as those of a simpleton, as one whose mind is disturbed. Sara cannot imagine freedom within these walls, in such low-ceilinged space ... and how often she tells me.

'Is a bear free in a cage, mistress?'

But I cannot now imagine freedom outside a cage. I can only imagine it here. So this has become my purpose.

'I am free,' I say again as another stone is forced into place with the thick plaster of animal hair and clay and, I confess, the temptation is to scream. It is not a new sight or a labour unknown, this walling. I have watched such labour before, house builders at work, building a wall ... but never with eyes inside; the view inside the coffin, as the lid is fitted tight. I am thirty-four years on this earth and alone in my cell, both a death and a coming home.

And here I pause, quite exhausted; one must concentrate on writing; truly, it is like hoeing a field.

*

82

Sara has departed, though the bishop has not.

She has hurried away with her worry and I kneel before the closing space and my disappearing door. I hear the chanting of the choir and the bishop's loud words, he is a loud man, there is a noise about him ... but I see only a little through the hole, which one final stone will fill and my sealed life begin. I see my mother. She stands slightly apart, solemn and locked in her face. I look at her: she is beautiful and separate in the sunlight.

I have not looked at her before, not in this manner; and she likes the crowd I think, and strikes a pose ... but her eyes are nervous, unsure as to others' thoughts, and therefore unsure of her own. I said goodbye this morning.

'I think you are a fool,' she says, 'but what can I do?'

'I wish you well, mother.'

'You wish me well and leave!'

'I can do no other.'

'And throw your name to the dogs!'

I do not wish for a fight; but there has been heaviness since my illness, since she declared me dead. We tried laughter about her words ... or I tried. It was kind laughter, for a chuckle can cheer and clear the soul. So on my recovery, I had made light of it.

'You closed my eyes, mother, but they wished to stay open!'

But my mother felt shame for naming her child a corpse while yet she lived. Her error scrawled a black mark against her name and she became resentful if mention was made of it. When a neighbour joked, 'Even your mother thought you dead!' she spoke harshly with them - and asked what right they had to speak of the matter?

83

'Nothing meant!' said the neighbour, 'nothing meant!' But like an archer with the arrow released, it could not be called back nor the wound undone.

My mother was quite blameless in the matter, and I told her so, for truly, my body had lost its will amid the fever, my mind drifting; and perhaps I imagined myself dead. As I say, I wished it so; death would have been relief, an end to the torment.

But since that day there had been a veil between us. And I see the uncertainty in her eyes and jaw. Do the crowd here praise her for bringing up such a daughter, so wedded to God? Or do they mock her for her loss, for losing a daughter in such a manner ... her only help in old age, now useless and separate in a cave?

My mother will both like the attention of this day; and not like it. She will like the crowd, the vigil, the robes, her importance in this moment, the attention upon her - but it must be good attention and not bad attention for my mother, or she turns to dark thoughts about herself and anger with those around.

'There are ways that are seemly,' she had said to me, on hearing my desire to become an anchoress. 'But this is unseemly. One's desires are not a trustworthy guide, Beatrix.'

'But godly desire?'

'We are not to trust desire - I say it plain, Beatrix, for desire is Satan's halter around our necks by which he tugs our lives to hell.'

'You must not be frightened of this change, mother.'

'Frightened? I am not frightened!'

'You sound frightened.'

'It is simply wrong! That is all I say ... quite wrong. And I will be proved right.'

She has resisted my calling – I name it so - like an angry crab from behind her shell.

'I cannot see the gain,' she said. 'Were there gain, I would not mind.' And then she sniffed loudly.

My mother says much with a sniff, wordless words ... and through the small hole now, I can see her wondering; I can see her in pain as she considers the nature of this public attention.

She would like a saint for a daughter, but not a fool; a fool will not reflect well on her. But others must decide which I am. They will decide the matter, she cannot decide for herself or know for herself, and I see her fear - a woman defined by the seeing of others.

Do I feel sorrow for her? I hope I feel compassion. She bears much, her daughter led away, the last rites spoken ... and never to see her or touch her again. But she has made me bear much as well; I feel this in my bones. And while she is against this journey, it is one I needs make. I do not argue with her, I have never chosen that path; she always has an answer and often it is harsh.

But neither, in my conscience, can I obey her. I have obeyed her with regard to chores, I have always done this; but we move apart like birds in the sky, choosing different space. There is much she cannot share in, so much of me she must deny and now - as the final stone is placed and she disappears from sight - like my Lord, I say 'Who is my mother?'

And here I pause. Sara is at my window; she has brought carrot soup. It is my first meal in this holy cave.

What adventures ahead?

Part Two

There is laughter outside my cell, laughter in the street. I like laughter, it cheers the spirit ... laughter is good. I believe Jesus laughed; he has laughed with me when we have spoken, though he does not laugh in church.

The merriment greets me in my cell where I am now an anchoress ... enclosed for life, stable of place with all wandering done, attached to St Julian's church. Only my bodily waste leaves, collected by Sara; I shall not leave until my body is too old and weak to carry my spirit anymore; and carried out then by another.

Do I ponder this too much? Some days I feel quite free, and some days I feel fear, concerned with what others might think, and my own worst judge, punishing myself. I have heard the anchoress stories; perhaps people tell them to frighten me. I hear of some burned in their cells; those who refused to leave, when pirates or marauding hoards looted and burned their towns. But we have good strong walls round Norwich. And there can be no leaving, whatever fiends arrive; even if the fiends are wild and dangerous men from France. Anyway, in my knowing, the worst fiends are not from France but live within myself; and so they are here already.

Sharing my space, I have a cat called Peter. He is black and white, with a little ginger about him and a large tail. I have sometimes stepped on him, unawares, and he complains; but more often I stroke him. Mr Curtgate advised that such a creature would be helpful. He has anxious eyes, Mr Curtgate, but a kind heart.

'He will mind the mice and the rats a little,' he tells me.

And on occasion, Peter catches them and Sara takes them away. I have a separate pot for their dead or dying bodies; they are not always quite killed. I have called him Peter for he reminds me of the saint, determined, whole-hearted but not always wise.

'And he will be company!' says Mr Curtgate, as though company is a thing I desire! Would I have chosen this path, if company was my aim? Hardly! But I believe he himself desires company and imagines me the same. Mistakenly, we believe others the same as ourselves. And I sometimes enjoy his sermons through the squint. He even read a gospel in English one Sunday, which caused a stir. After my weekly confession, I did ask him of this.

'Latin is the true way for scripture, of course,' he tells me. 'In order for its mystery to be maintained. But some say we might now hear a little in English to our profit.'

'And there are such manuscripts? Versions of the scriptures in English?'

'There are, yes.' His throat tightens a little as he speaks, but I am excited, I have never imagined such a thing; as if scripture could somehow blend with the tongue of the market place.

'They do exist,' said Mr Curtgate, glancing to both his left and right. 'But they are not - definitely not - for the eyes of the people. I keep the English version locked away.'

I do not see him through the squint, I have pulled the curtain; but I know he sweats.

'Do you have such a bible?' I ask.

'We will not talk of these things, Julian.'

'Indeed ... but do you?'

'You are shriven - now go in peace.'

＊

And with or without Peter, I have company enough. I do not feel I lack company with the noise of the harbour hammers, the carts and the boatmen shouting; they shout a great deal, the carpenter bawling at his apprentice, like he once bawled at Richard.

And then different voices - the voices of the troubled, as they come to my window. Yes, the anguish of Norwich does arrive somewhat, simple folk begging prayer and counsel for their lives; though I ask Sara to mind the flow, or else I become flooded by them, I become too crowded here, where I came to be alone.

'You retreat to be alone and sudden all want to see you, mistress!'

Yesterday, a woman appeared at my window, Maud Sadler, and complained to me of God. She tells me her prayers are not answered. I do not see her, the curtain between us, but she is distressed and blaming herself. She complains of God, but really blames herself - and what am I to say? I am not much trained in this.

'He don't answer me and I blames myself, I do! I'm not proper enough, not proper like the other folk - and now look at me!' I sit quiet for a while, for listening needs silence. 'You still there?' she asks.

'I am here, my friend. I just ponder.'

'Oh. Well, I don't know where pondering'll get us!'

I tell her we often feel as barren after our prayers, as we did before them. I say this is quite usual and no sin. 'And we might believe God's silence is caused by our folly; I have felt this myself.'

'I try to lead a good life, anyways,' she says.

'And God sees only your good, Maud, be sure of that. Your good is all God sees.'

'I hardly think so. I accuse myself every day, every day I do, so what must God think?'

'He says 'Accuse not yourself much too much.'

'Oh he does, does he?'

'He says you are not to accuse yourself much too much, thinking that your tribulation and woe are your own fault, for they are not your own fault.'

'Well whose fault are they but my own?'

'They are not your fault, not your fault at all - can you believe that?' She is quiet for a moment, perhaps surprised. 'These things are not your fault, Maud, for I tell you, and this is the truth, that whatever you do here on earth, whether good or bad, you will have woes. Life is difficult, though we do our best, we start from there.'

How I know this ...

'And who says such things?'

'Jesus says this.'

'Jesus?!'

She almost chokes.

'Jesus said it to me.'

I will not pretend otherwise.

'Jesus said it to you? No wonder they sealed you in!'

'Jesus said these things to me quite clearly, some years back, but I do not forget.' I stay calm though she mocks. 'So I say them to you, Maud, as he said them to me: you must not accuse yourself. But also ... we must not pray for everything.'

'Your meaning?'

I fear she tires of me.

'We must pray only for God's will, Maud. We must pray not for everything to be as we wish ... but only for God's will to be done.'

She pauses.

'Is not the life of my child God's will, Mistress Julian?'

'Your child?'

I am stopped, as if hit by a pole. It is her child who ails, her child who she prays for ... and her child who will likely die. I am silent before this severe mystery. I say I will pray that all shall be well with her.

'So how did you feel then?' she asks.

'Of what do you speak?' I am confused.

'When your own daughter died? When your own daughter was taken, and lay all lifeless and cold. How did you feel, Mistress Julian?'

She appears to know my story; and perhaps I wish she did not.

'I looked upon the cross for consolation,' I say, hardening a little.

'And did it help?'

'Did it help? In the end,' I say, 'in the end.'

And there I pause, because I cannot go on. I sense dissonance in my being ... shallow, untruthful words. I do not speak the truth, for my child was everything - and is that why she was taken? Because her life was not God's will?

In truth, the cross did not help in those days. And now there is neither peace nor prayer on my lips as, with my visitor gone, I lie on the rushes by the altar, gazing up.

I am quite empty of virtue.

*

Richard and Lettice have returned in my dreams of late; I do not know why. Memories return, those difficult days return, and they return without meaning. I cannot be grateful, yet I cannot let go; I cannot cheer them or be merry with them; yet neither can I weep. As I say, they arise without meaning, they tighten my chest, I struggle to breathe.

And beyond, in the city, the plague comes and goes; it seems the monster is sated for now. When it will return, I do not know. But whatever occurs, whatever unfolding awaits us, it has left us desolate and weeping with its fever and boils; and in some manner, I believe it has killed us all ... even those who live. We are glad that we live and yet we are not. For what kindness does it leave behind?

I remember the friar speaking - though his words are still a scar.

'God has his quiver full of arrows,' he announced to our hunched gathering. 'A quiver full of pestilence, fevers and all manner of diseases! He shoots them into our friends, our families, ourselves! And none but himself can pull them out! We must pray harder!'

But what to pray when we do not know what is wrong? And who are we to pray to - if God aims his arrows at us? And if this is judgement, what is the sin? Idleness, drunkenness, gossip? Some say so. Yet if these were the target, were they worth such terrible darts?

I look around. Monk and whore, child and drunkard, rich and poor, courteous and cruel, Richard and Lettice, my father ... they all die.

Truly, I need a mind greater than mine to explain such things; for the mind of the church does not lead us far, if it can speak only of arrows. And anyway, I do not know this bowman they speak of. I have never seen this wild man with his quiver, so full of violent darts, and released with uncurious intent.

And I feel anger, which I do not wish to feel; I know not where to put it and I believe I might scream. I am stretched on the floor; I lie on my back, looking up through the smoke hole, wishing to become smoke, to be freed from this body.

Though in truth, it is my spirit which sighs through my body. It is my spirit which grieves in my body, not my body itself; and what gain in freedom from this body if my spirit remains un-mended?

I hate my three windows; they seem to oppress me.

*

'You forget the fourth window,' says Sister Lucy, after silence.

I do not know what she means.

Lucy comes from Carrow Abbey, she is my spiritual guide, my straightener; and we speak of spiritual things. She says she guides me from error, though whether I err I do not know. I do not feel I err, though I have complained a great deal today. I have spoken harshly of my fellow Christians, finding much fault with them all - as if I have a list of grievances, well remembered. These people bring me trouble.

'You do not like those who come to your windows?' says Sister Lucy.

'I begin to hate the windows,' I say.

'You hate the windows?'

'They are like three terrors, Sister Lucy - gaunt-eyed holes, they judge me and expose me. Yet they will not move and they will not go away. So what am I to do?'

She looks at me but does not help me, when I need help. She continues to stare.

'You forget the fourth window,' she says, after silence.

I do not know what she means.

'I see only three,' I say.

'And I see four ... for I see you, Julian.'

'Me?'

'You are the fourth window, through which you espy the other three. Is this not so? Look after the fourth window and the other three will look after themselves.'

I speak up for myself. How can I not?

'I try to please - what more can I do? I try and please everyone! But some people will not be pleased!'

'And why do you try to please?'

'Well, it is the right attitude, surely? It is right to please others. Surely this is God's will?'

And surely she knows this? Yet Sister Lucy just smiles. I remember the smile from the abbey, like sunlight in winter; and it is homely to see it again.

'It is only the terror in you which tries to please, Julian.'

'The *windows* are the terror, as I told you.'

'No, no - you are the terror, Julian. There is terror in you - and I would wish it gone.'

I find my eyes watering a little at these words, for they are true.

'I just try and please.'

And now I weep, the tears break; I can take no more.

'As you say, as you say,' says Sister Lucy, kindly. 'But there is no need. Little Beatrix can be calm. She does not now need the "yes" of others. She has grown into Julian, a substantial woman; substantial in spirit.'

'But if I do not please, what then will they think of me?'

'The perceptions of others are a prison, Julian; so do not lock yourself inside them. Care rather for what you think of yourself; for you are the fourth window, through which all things are seen. If there is a scar in this glass, then all things are scarred.' She pauses. 'But all shall be well, Julian, I know this - all shall be well.'

And though I oft hear these words, common parlance as they are, today I believe them, and know them to be true.

All shall be well. I feel the terror dissolving.

'The fourth window, Julian, is the window that needs looking after.'

9

It feels wonderful to my touch.

After my confession, when I do not know what to say, Mr Curtgate offers me a book through the Christ window. I take it and enjoy the feel of the leather.

'This is the book we spoke of,' he says. 'The *Ancrene Wisse*. It is your rule book.'

He speaks as though I must have a rule book to live by; and perhaps he is right. The *Ancrene Wisse* is a rule of life for the anchoress. It tells what we should and should not do. We spoke of it before I entered the cell.

'I think love is the only rule,' I said.

'But love needs strong fences to protect it,' replied Mr Curtgate quickly.

'As long as the fences are not too many or too high, Mr Curtgate. I do not believe in a God of fences.'

'It was written in the last century as a guide for three sisters of gentle birth,' he explains. 'Three sisters who sought the life of an anchoress.'

He had not mentioned the book again ... until now.

'I think you will find it helpful,' he says.

'Oh, I will,' I say. 'I will.' I am excited in the main to hold a book written in English; this is my thrill. I care less for the rules it gives and will not detain you with them. It decrees that the cell of an anchoress should have three windows, and these I have described. (Though sometimes drunk men shout through them, and seek things other than counsel.) We are advised, however, to be careful of our windows, lest we imagine more importance than we possess.

"My dear sisters, love your windows as little as you ever can," reads Mr Curtgate from the rule book. "All the misery that there now is, and ever yet was, and ever shall be – it all comes of sight."

I do not know if this is so. Perhaps the author's sight leads him towards trouble, but my sight does not. Instead, I learn that the greatest fiends are within me and therefore quite beyond sight, lurking in the shadows within. In obedience, however, I curtain my windows, thick and black, lest my seeing leads me astray.

"And wear no iron or haircloth or hedgehog skins," reads Mr Curtgate. He appears concerned about this. "And do not beat yourself therewith, neither with a scourge nor leather thongs." You will not do this, will you, Beatrix?'

'Julian.'

'Julian, yes. The rule book is most clear on this matter.'

'I do not believe God looks on me more kindly for the wearing of hedgehog skins.'

He does not sense my laughter.

'Then in this matter you are wise,' he says. 'Very wise'

'And in others?'

I jest with him; but again, Mr Curtgate is not for jesting.

"They who love most shall be most blessed," he adds, reading again. 'This is what the book says. "Not they who lead the most austere life - for love outweighs this."'

'I believe so utterly. No hedgehogs and no thongs.'

Mr Curtgate seems reassured.

'And you will eat?'

'I will eat.'

'There are women across the seas who starve themselves to God's glory, it is the new spiritual way among some. But the *Ancrene Wisse* warns against such behaviour, against such punishment of the self. I merely say this.'

'Simplicity but not punishment,' I say.

'Quite so,' says Mr Curtgate. 'Simplicity without punishment.' He seems to like my phrase, which pleases me. I believe I can find a phrase.

'If God finds no wrong in me and no cause for blame – then what purpose is there in harming myself? I imagine God must cry at such doings.'

Mr Curtgate is suddenly unhappy. Have I said something amiss?

'I don't believe we can speak of God crying, Julian.'

'Did not Jesus weep for Lazarus?' I ask.

'Yes ... but, well - it is best you keep these things private.' He is uncomfortable.

'Best that I keep scripture private?'

'Best you withdraw from the world, keep in your cell, and speak not of such things, unless in private devotion.'

I tell him I do not withdraw from the world.

'Norwich still flows around me and through me, Mr Curtgate ... like a river. I cannot now see the city, but I can hear it, speak with it ... and smell it at my door!'

And sadly, I feel it still in my body; I might have said this also. For yes, I still feel Mr Strokelady, he does not leave. My body knows him even now ... and I wish this were not so. He has returned to me often of late, in my spirit, and it is a matter of discomfort. He has no place here in the cell, yet in some manner he is here; though I am free, he traps me.

And the fiends still come. They come at my throat and in my woman's parts, they try to strangle me, to lessen me, to shame me, their heat and their stench, quite vile; they terrify and torment, jabbering and muttering in different voices.

"'True anchoresses are indeed birds of heaven,'" continues Mr Curtgate, reading again. "'They fly up high and sit singing merrily on the green boughs.'"

And here I pause, feeling unworthy; I do not always sing merrily. And I wonder if Mr Strokelady will ever come to my window? I wonder if he lives here still, prowling the city.

And if he does arrive, with a cheery 'Good morning!' then what do I say? No rule book or green bough will help me then.

*

The rule book says I am not to converse with men, unless observed, lest I am tempted. I do not keep this rule. I am not tempted and further, I do not warm to its spirit, though today, perhaps, I change my mind.

'Mistress Julian, are you there?'

I hear his voice at my window of counsel. It is not a voice I know ... a man's voice and furtive, as if he comes in the night; though I have barely finished Terce ... and I do not wish to speak with him. I received two visitors yesterday who are sufficient for the week. As the rule book says, I must not fall in love with the window, with being desired for my counsel ... a puffed up and needy soul.

'You must speak with Sara Heady if you wish to converse with me, sir. She will give you a time.'

'But we have time now.'

'You have time; I do not. We shall speak another time, when you have spoken to Sara Heady; so please go from my cell.'

But he does not go and he feels too close, I sense him beyond the curtain.

'Does God not wish for you to help people?'

'He wishes for them to speak first with Sara.'

I do not know this, but hope that it is so.

'But Mistress Julian, this will be to your benefit.'

'My benefit is God.'

'To your financial benefit.'

'My benefit is God.'

'That you might have food enough to live and pray ... and quills enough to write.'

'Who spoke of quills? Or writing?'

I do not wish this known.

'I desire no trouble for you, believe me. I simply need your kind assistance.'

'Then speak with Sara ...'

'I wish only to leave some loved possessions with you, and is that so bad? I wish to leave them with you while I travel. It is no sin to be careful. I believe God wills us all to be careful.'

I pause, understanding his plea. I have heard of such practice before: the anchoress is asked to store valuables, when people go away, for there is no place safer in these troubled times than an anchorite cell; and money is given to the anchoress in exchange for such keeping.

'Place them under the matting in your home,' I say, for I do not desire this invasion. 'Straw and earth will be your strong box.'

'I would like a securer holding, in case of trouble.'

'I do not want the company of your possessions, kind sir; I wish to be alone.'

'Of course, of course, a godly calling!' he mutters. 'But these things are worth a great deal, they are of value to me, of great personal worth.' A soft hand, not the hand of a labourer, comes through the curtain and opening its palm, reveals a large precious stone, the colour of red wine. 'And there are many others such as this, Mistress Julian, of too high a price to be hidden at home.'

'Take your hand from my cell, please.' I say this firmly.

'I merely show you the worth of what I propose.'

I am disgusted by his pushing hand.

'Your hand invades my home. Please take it away.'

'I only meant ...'

'Take it out!'

I feel this advance in my body; my chest tightens at the sight of it, this uninvited arm.

'I would pay you well for your safe keeping.'

I turn away in distress, unprepared for my anger and - may I be forgiven - with no love for this Christian man. And I am wishing Sara were here, she would chase him away. I face the squint, desiring him gone.

And then a strange noise behind me, a screech followed by loud cursing. My visitor is cursing! Peter lands by my feet, crying out, thrown down to the ground and I turn to see the invading arm and hand being withdrawn ...withdrawn in haste, teeth and claw marks displayed, a little blood.

'Satan's cat!' shouts the man. 'Call yourself a Christian, woman? Rot in hell, you whore! You'll have nothing from me! I'll see you starve!'

And I am disturbed by the visit, discomfort lingers. I breathe a little, and my breathing is a friend. I feel the relief of his departure, for I know him to be gone. Though perhaps his threat is true, perhaps he can harm me ... who knows the power of this rude fellow? Will I starve in this place? I know I cannot leave it.

I ponder these things, while Peter licks his paw; he is hurt in the fall. He limps to his place by the altar, where I lay straw for him. He settles there, licking his leg; but I cannot settle, made unsafe by events. I pray to God, but feel only my weakness and lack of courteous love for my visitor; for if a man or woman ceases to love any of their fellow Christians, then they love none, this is so; for the unloving of one is the unloving of all, and such a person is not saved in that moment, for they are not at peace ... and I am not at peace.

And from within, the voice of the fiend declares me a fool, and a fool I am, unworthy of this calling and due only the contempt of heaven.

And here I pause, the daughter of shame. I shall not eat tonight.

10

I have replied to Mr Ball. He wishes to meet and I have agreed. Have I been wise in this agreement? They say he is the most dangerous man in England.

And yes, as you see, I write again, having rested my quills and ink for some while.

I note my discomfort when last I put ink on this parchment: the arm forced through the window, the jewel held in the sweating palm, the sense of attack. It was a storm in its moment, a strong feeling ... yet strange how now I forget the storm; how one thing takes the place of another and how our Lord's healing arrives out of sight, a stealthy appearance.

Mr Curtgate has heard of Mr Ball's visit, I do not know how; and he does not speak of him with enthusiasm.

'He is excommunicated,' he says through the squint. He has brought me the bread and the wine, and we talk after; though he becomes anxious at mention of John Ball. 'A few months past - he was excommunicated.' I know this is not good; it is a word of terror. 'By the Pope. This man who comes to see you is excluded from the sacraments and services of the Christian church, you understand this? And consigned to hell unless he repents.' He speaks with haste and impatience. 'Do we really wish him here, at this window? The Bishop will not be pleased, and that is a mild telling.'

'And what is Mr Ball to repent of?'

I feel no haste, and am a little sly; for I know what he says, having heard him in the fields outside the abbey. He did not hide his thoughts beneath that sky and spoke most clear. But I wish better to know Mr Curtgate; to hear his private thoughts.

'He preaches in favour of ecclesiastical poverty; for less wealth in the church and for the equality of all people - this is his cause.'

'He sounds like you, Mr Curtgate.'

I do hear echoes of such things in his sermons.

'He does not sound like me!'

'I speak only as I hear.'

Sara also has concerns; for Mr Ball is the talk of the city.

'You do not wish to be speaking to his sort,' she says, on hearing of his coming. 'I don't know why you are; and really, I don't.'

'He wrote to me and asked. A boy both delivered it and took my reply.'

'Visitors should come through me.'

'I know. For some reason he chose otherwise, Sara.'

'I'm sure he did, the little toad.'

And I wonder again why Sara was there that day, in the field outside the abbey, listening to this 'toad'.

'I could hardly turn him away,' I say.

'And I say, you don't want to hang with him.'

'Why would he hang?'

'He will hang ...he'll feel the rope and feel his neck stretched. I have heard the stories - and they are true.'

'What sort of stories?'

I learn to ask questions for myself, rather than step inside the judgements of others, which I often find to be a house with no roof.

'It is forbidden to hear him preach, mistress. So if you speak with him ...'

'Who forbids?'

'The Archbishop of Canterbury! It is the archbishop who forbids him ... and imprisons him.'

'You seem well stuffed with news, Sara.'

'I make it my business to be stuffed, with you fastened to this place, like a trapped rabbit.'

'You used to call me a trapped bear. Do I get smaller?'

'No, but this world becomes more mad - it is quite so, believe me. It was read out at St Michael's. The archbishop has made it against the law even to listen to John Ball.'

'They must fear him greatly. I believe I fear him - and we have not even met!'

'Even to *listen* to him. Do you hear what I say, Mistress Julian? Even to listen to him is against the law.'

She calls me thus when annoyed.

'I hear it well, Sara, you say it thrice. Mother Church has her reasons, I'm sure ...'

There is a pause. I hear her with her buckets.

'Though if all this was meant to frighten Mr Ball, all these threats - then it hasn't worked!' she says - 'hasn't worked at all!' I sense a different tone. Does she now warm to him? I hear a smile in her words. 'I'm told he preaches to even more folk these days; becomes the more interesting for the ban.'

'Maybe he also speaks true.'

'Maybe he does, who can say?'

'But where does he preach, if he cannot preach in church?'

I confess, and may the Lord forgive me, I continue to pretend unknowing.

'He stands in a field, Mistress Julian, with the hedges for friends.'

'Our Lord preached on a hillside.'

'Well, I don't say he is Jesus! But he does stand in a field and there they gather, in Ashen, Billericay and Bocking; in Braintree, Cressing Temple, Dedham, Coggeshall, Fobbing, Goldhanger, Great Baddow, Little Henny, Stisted, Waltham ...'

'And Norwich?'

I confess I wish to stop her listing. I know there are lists in scripture, but those are holy lists. This is a mere list of towns and I tire of it. But I wish also to find out her interest.

'I hear so.'

'You sound as you admire him somewhat.'

'I hardly admire him, mistress. It's not my place to admire or otherwise.'

'Is it not?'

'I just say what he does ... and then wonder that you should wish to see him, being as he is now a twice-imprisoned enemy of the Church - which might make the same of you.'

'Yet you heard him speak in Norwich.'

I hear her gasp a little.

'Who says so?'

'I beheld you, Sara ... for I was there too.'

'You were there? Have you been playing the fool with me?'

'No, no! I was on my way back from the abbey ... I could hardly not be there.'

'Yet you stopped and listened?'

'I did, yes.'

'Then you must be careful, mistress, very careful.'

'Well, I won't be hearing him preach when he comes,' I say, wishing now to be alone. 'He merely comes to talk.'

'They say as he always preaches, that John Ball - even when he's not preaching, he's preaching. He can't help himself. He opens his mouth and he starts preaching.'

Sara seems to be all a-worry again, and eager to give her worry to me; like one passing a hot stick from the fire, quickly tossed into hands close by. So it is we pass our worry to others.

'I do not turn people away, Sara - such judgement is not kind. Christians come to my window without judgement. I do not ask them whether they are worthy. If I asked if they were worthy, I would speak with no one, for no one imagines themselves so. Yet I believe them all to be worthy. If Satan's less pleasant brother appeared, I believe I would have to converse!'

'It may not be kind, mistress - but perhaps it is wise. Maybe turning away from Mr Ball is wise.'

'Wise as the serpent is wise?'

'Wise towards staying alive.'

'And what is life if it is not kind? That is fool's wisdom.'

'The Church says he is a plague to the soul. This is what they say.'

'I know the power of the plague, Sara.'

I am caught out. My eyes moisten with memory, my breathing is disturbed. I feel again like the little girl with her father lost, when I cried a deep well of tears. How I cried! The River Yare should have burst its banks, trading boats rocked in the flood ... merchants demanding the girl calm herself or muffle her bubbling blubbing eyes ... I wept a torrent of tears ...

But now I wonder: is Mr Ball truly such a plague on our souls? No one believes I should meet him; all ease me away ... and I find myself troubled by a man I have not met. I think of him tonight, out there in the dark. Does this Hedge Priest rest happily tonight? Does he know what happy is?

He comes soon to Norwich, it seems. I have told him to arrive by night.

11

'Why are those whom we call lords, masters over us? That is my question, mistress!'

The voice through my curtain is insistent; it batters the cloth. While Norwich sleeps, my visitor talks. I wonder if he ever sleeps. He means to save this world, and if force of word and argument can do so, then Mr Ball will surely be our saviour.

'How do they deserve it, the bishops and Lords? How do they deserve such elevation?' I feel his face leaning towards me. 'And by what right on earth or in heaven do they keep the rest of us enslaved and trampled upon?'

He does not wait for an answer, Mr Ball. Some wait for response, to sense your feeling. But Mr Ball does not see the need.

'We, who are descended from Adam and Eve! We, who share their parentage! We share their parentage - do you believe so, Mistress Julian?'

'I believe so, yes.'

'So how are they better than us in social degree? When at the beginning we were of equal birth, and quite level in every way? Were we not created equal?'

The reputation of Mr Ball does not lie. He does preach, even when speaking at a curtained window; he debates, he prods and he preaches. His gaolers must have had a hard time of it; I do not imagine he quietened behind their bars.

'Perhaps we have different parts to play,' I say.

I must hope so, for I cannot do as he does. I cannot shout and press like him.

'If God willed that there should be serfs, he would have declared so at the beginning of the world. This is all I say. There would have been serfs in paradise! Did you note serfs in Eden when last you visited?'

I do not know how to respond. I ask if he comes to drown me in words, for this he has done, and he sorrows at this. He says he does not come to drown me, not at all; this is the last thing he wishes. He seeks counsel, he says – he seeks kind words and counsel; though whether there is room in him for counsel, I do not know. He appears a man sure in all things.

'We are formed in Christ's likeness, Mistress Julian, you cannot deny this.'

'Why would I wish to, Mr Ball? You are hardly the first ...'

'Yet they do not *treat* us like Christ; they treat us like animals.'

'They treated Christ in similar fashion, Mr Ball ... they crucified him, his blood thick on his body and drying to a crust.'

He speaks as if they treated our Lord kindly, as if only the peasant suffers, when our Lord suffers every day. But he comes back at me.

'And because Christ was so treated, he wishes others to be treated the same? Is this what you say, mistress?'

'No ...'

'That we are all to be crucified now by the king? That we are to be whipped daily and say thank you?' He pauses only for a moment. 'You know this to be so, Mistress Julian.'

'I know what to be so?'

'The unfairness, here in Norwich.' He slows a little. 'It is the same in Colchester, the same in Maidstone ... the same in London. Everywhere the same, the story is the same, they dress in velvet and furs, while we wear cloth. They enjoy wine and spices and the finest bread - while we have rye bread and water. Is this as God intends?'

'He enfolds us in his love, I know this.'

'And how will he do this if we starve or fall down exhausted ... or feel our skulls cracked by their blows? Is this love?'

'He will help us up.'

'Who will help us up?'

'God will help us ... like a kind Lord helping his servant to his feet.'

But this thought is strange to him; I do not feel it heard.

'A kind lord?! You must fish in a different pond from me, Mistress Julian. Do you meet many kind lords on your way to the market?'

'I speak of my vision ...'

'They have their fine houses and manors. I passed your bishop's palace, the bishop who chases me - he lives in luxury, while we brave wind and rain, toiling in the fields. It is by the sweat of our brows they maintain their high state.'

'The bishop does not go without; we find agreement there.'

'And it's not the rich who pay for their luxury; it's the poor who pay for their luxury - they ask the poor to pay for their wine! And crush them in court if they do not.'

'The lawyers. Surely they ...'

'Lawyers!? They open their mouths for a fee, but not for charity. It is easier to measure the mist than get an unpaid word out of them ... only with gold on the table do they remember their speech. They help no one but themselves.'

Mr Ball speaks strong words, and I do not know how to reply. I wish to speak of our kind and courteous God; and he wishes to speak of the desperate poor.

'You're silent again,' he says to me. He struggles to trust my presence behind the curtain. Perhaps he simply struggles to trust.

'You must allow some silence,' I say. 'I am perhaps more familiar with silence than you.'

I do not imagine much silence in his head; it is as though an angry rat lives there.

'You think it right that the poor die, Mistress Julian?'

'I have near-died myself, Mr Ball ... and found there the greatest grace.'

'That is no answer, and really it is not.'

His words chill me.

'We are not always given answers, Mr Ball, this I discover.'

'There is no grace in what is done to the poor - only harm.'

'There is grace in paradise and I believe it spills over the earth.'

He shuffles.

'Well, I don't feel much spillage when the harvest is bad and the children wide-eyed with hunger.'

I feel his face come closer to the window and his voice drops a little; he speaks as if to a child. And perhaps he thinks me as such; I felt this with the bishop and do not warm to it.

'Things cannot go well in England,' he says, 'nor shall they ever go well - there can be no grace, this is what I say - till all land and all wealth be held in common. I believe this, Mistress Julian; till there be but one condition for us all.'

'You do not like hierarchy, Mr Ball.'

'It is God who shunned it, not I. It is he who shunned it there in Eden!' He returns to Eden, where Adam and Eve stood equal. And I feel the force of these words.

'Perhaps Eden is lost.'

'Yet it remains in our hearts, Julian, and lives in our minds, the thought that things might be better - no gentleman there, no fine robes, no meat for one but not the other. So why is it so on earth?'

'I do not know. Perhaps it is to test us ...'

'We share the Eucharist - but we share nothing else! It is an abomination!'

'You are an angry man, Mr Ball.'

And I feel pinioned by his rage; it crashes and disturbs like the thunder.

'I believe our Lord was angry. And perhaps you are too, mistress ...'

'My name is Julian.'

'And perhaps that is why you hide yourself away; to keep your anger unseen and yourself safe from them.'

'I do not hide myself away.'

'You do not hide yourself away?!' I hear him laugh a little, in scorn. 'Then why do I speak to you through a curtained window? You want no part of this world, no part of this bondage, this pomp and poverty - we are not so different.'

'I believe we are a little different.'

I cannot say, 'We are the same,' for it is not so.

'You are not angry?' he asks.

'Angry at what?'

'Angry at *this*! At everything which surrounds you in your hideaway. Or do you imagine this city and this country suddenly sunny and fair?'

'I do not hide away.' I do not like it when he speaks like this. 'And I am not absent. This city passes through me, I feel it; each day it makes its way through my soul.'

I do not choose anger, it is true; though what I feel towards Mr Strokelady - perhaps I call that anger. And it sticks in my throat, blocking my voice, like a rag in a drain, this I have come to know ... but should I forgive him now? One cannot blame forever. And then the bishop: is there anger in me towards him? He does not understand my intentions and speaks across me, as if I am a fool, something lesser to him - as if men must know things better ... though he helped me to this place, when he might have said 'No'. So is this anger?

And then I consider my mother. She has done her best, and not without difficulties along the way; so maybe it is not anger I feel, for what does anger achieve? The more I think, the less I know ... though I find myself stirred in the presence of Mr Ball, and discomforted.

'There are feelings other than anger, Mr Ball.'

He chuckles.

'Without anger, they are pretend feelings ... like lace hiding a stain on the table.'

'I do not believe our Lord is so angry. I met a suffering Jesus in my visions. He suffered most grievously - blood in thick red rivulets streaming down his sweet face ... but not an angry man. He was a figure of love, which is surely different.'

'You don't believe our Lord angry?' He is up from his seat. 'You imagine he smashed the money lender's tables and the money lenders themselves because he was cheerful? The cheerful do not smash tables and people in the temple - the angry do these things. We should try it in the cathedral and watch the bishop's face. He will not call it love! And I might so do on leaving here!'

'You must not do that, Mr Ball. You must leave quietly.'

'So no one knows I have knocked on your door? I heard better things of you.'

This man exists in a manner which I do not. I have never felt such force in anyone, and this without sight of the man. He is a powerful soul, a disturbance in the world, and I cannot disagree. I wish all people fed and no one abused; and I struggle for words.

'"You shall not be overcome,"' I say, simply. 'These words were spoken to me.'

He is silent ... for the first time, as if his quiver is empty of arrows, with nothing left to shoot.

'My life is not an easy life, Mistress Julian.' I hear his eyes watering; I hear it in his voice, the approach of tears. I hear him also wipe his nose. 'I am denied my church and forced to preach to the sky.'

'Though many gather beneath it to hear you.'

'They gather because they starve and no one else hears them; no one else names them, while their children die and the friars get fat.'

'You must be careful, Mr Ball.'

'I cannot be careful. I will never be careful while dark power rules this world; though I break and break again ... and see heavy clouds ahead.'

'"You shall not be overcome." I say it again to you, Mr Ball. It is the assurance and comfort of God against all tribulations that may arise.'

There is silence and I wonder if he sobs; I believe I hear so.

'I do not feel comfort, Mistress Julian ... though I thank you for your prayers.'

'I have not given you my prayers.'

'Then for your kindly thoughts.'

'I neither offer you prayer nor kindly thought. I offer only the Lord's words to me; the words given to me. '

'The clouds ...'

'He did not say "You shall not be perturbed," Mr Ball.'

'No.'

'He did not say you shall not be troubled or distressed.'

'I know both those.'

'But he did say "You shall not be overcome."'

'I shall not be overcome?'

I reach through the window, parting the curtain a little and find his arm, well-haired and layered with the sweat and grime of the journey.

'You shall not be overcome.'

I feel him take my wrist and lift it a little. He kisses my hand, rough stubble on my skin and then he is letting it go and slowly, I bring it back inside my cell and gaze on it a moment ... a hand baptised in his tears, my hand is wet.

And I know he is gone; there is no one now behind the curtain. I know when another is there ... and Mr Ball is gone.

I pause in my confusion, my peat fire burning; my heart pounds and my questions rise with the smoke.

12

S ara believes I need more cheer, and perhaps I do;
for something is lost in my soul. Is my early joy
disappeared? It may secretly have left.

Mr Ball, who I wrote of, is long gone and I know not
how he fares; though he has left a mark in my being. I
feel a dullard in this door-less cave, where once I felt
free. I feel as a rabbit trapped, today I feel so - a creature ensnared. I can perform nothing here and I am
oppressed by this thought, held as a prisoner by these
walls, a prison I chose. But was it the choice of a fool?

Mr Curtgate spoke of this when we conversed in
the graveyard.

'You wish to live in a cell, but do you know what you
ask for? Perhaps your dream will prove troublesome!'

He said I could know nothing until my dream was
endured awhile ... and told me how an anchoress in Suf-
folk threw herself against her walls unto death.

'Most sad, most sad.'

And I said to him, I remember saying, that I would
need only God.

'I need only God, Mr Curtgate.'

And this is true, it is still true, I do need only God; though something inside me withers, like the leaves on a dying tree. I have lost some joy and feel the observations of Mr Ball sharply. He spoke of three needs when we met. He said there were three graces to be shared in common by all: the grace of clothing, to protect from cold; the grace of food, to prevent hunger and the grace of drink, for when your throat is dry.

I rely on these graces myself. Yet all I could speak of was another grace: God's love. But what is such love if you starve?

He told me how we must be earthy in our care, and halt injustice.

'Peasants are forced to work for free on church land! They must work church land without wage for two days a week - which keeps them from their own! They cannot work on their own land ... which means they cannot grow enough food for their families! Is this right, Mistress Julian?'

'It sounds harsh, though perhaps there is reason ...'

'Oh, there's reason all right - and the reason is injustice! Yet this is what the Church does, Mistress Julian, it takes food from the children – and then sends the money to the Pope in his palace!'

I remember Mr Curtgate's words about English money draining away to Rome.

Mr Ball believes peasants should be free of this burden - a burden that makes the church richer, but the poor poorer. And is he right? I do not know if he is right, I feel him to be right. Yet here I live in a cell attached to the church he hates - like a louse on a rat, feeding daily.

And that is not all that stays from the visit of Mr Ball. He called this cell a hideaway, as though I hide here from the world.

'You have a good hideaway here, Mistress Julian, safe from the troubles of the world!'

And the bishop spoke with similar words, his first remark when I entered the palace. He inquired whether the world was too grievous for me, I remember this, as if I did not have the substance to stand in this world; as if I must hide away, like a child frightened by a storm ... like one too weak.

'Let's be having Stinky,' says Sara through the window. This is what she calls waste. She arrives early, and perhaps it is good; for I think to excess and find myself kidnapped by worry.

'Your thoughts abduct you,' as Sister Lucy once said. 'And take you to no good place.' And I do think too much, particularly where a slight or a worry is concerned. So I cover the chamber pot with a cloth and pass it through the window, letting go of my sins as Christ would have me do.

'How do you fare?' I ask Sara. She pretends not to hear. 'Do you fare well?'

'Best not worry about me, Mistress Julian.' Sara will not have any person worry about her; she forbids it, though still I ask.

'I do not worry, Sara, I merely wonder. To worry and to wonder are not the same.'

'Well, you must merely wonder about something else. My leg heals so I can't complain.' I do not know about her leg. 'I'll be dancing soon and I've brought a little barley broth and - because you need cheering - some dried herring. You like dried herring.'

The basket is passed through Sara's window. I do like dried herring.

'I feast like a king.'

'A king would eat more than once a day, mistress. And drink wine with his supper.'

'I am not your mistress, Sara.' I tire of saying this ... I have said it again and again. I remind her occasionally, but it makes no difference. 'And you did not tell me of your leg.'

'Nothing to tell.'

'So tell me of this nothing.'

'Accidents happen. And I don't think I'm worth your prayers, mistress.'

'And what if I think you are?'

'Pray for the king.'

I am surprised.

'The king? Does he struggle in his duties?'

'I don't know. I'm not the queen.'

I laugh ... and Sara likes it that I laugh.

'You're my queen, Sara.' And now I wonder. 'Who is the king?'

'The one next to the queen,' says Sara. 'Used to be Edward - until the syphilis got him.'

'How do you know that, Sara?'

I do not know where Sara hears things, or how she hears them; though I believe her uncle was once in the bishop's employ, serving at high table and hearing talk.

'It's what they say.'

Perhaps I do not know enough of the world ... though perhaps I know enough. The world is full of noise.

'God does not change with the news,' I say. 'And maybe we should not either; for the news is always a storm ... or so my mother would say.'

'"Always a storm,"' she'd say. '"And storms bring nothing good."' Do you see my mother, Sara?'

'I don't, mistress, no.'

'She does not visit me.'

'No.'

'But I will ask Mr Curtgate, he will know about the king. I will ask him.'

'I am told he's only a boy.'

I do believe she knows more than she says.

'The king is a boy? So you do know, Sara?'

'As I say - a little here and there.'

'And his name?'

'What does the king's name matter? When all he does is stamp on our necks.'

'His name?'

'It may be Richard.'

'Then I shall pray for him, our boy king Richard, as we are asked to do - and I will pray for you, Sara.'

I hear Sara busying herself with matters. She goes outside to empty the chamber pot, down to the street ... and there is quiet. But she is not gone, for she returns quickly making work for herself.

'And Mr Ball came to see you, I suppose?' she asks, with a voice that pretends not to care.

'He came a while ago.'

'Really?'

'Yes. He came at night ... and left the city unhindered, I believe.'

Does she wish to hear of our conversation? She does not ask after others who I counsel. But she does ask after Mr Ball.

'And you spoke?'

'We spoke.'

'It's not for me to ask what you spoke of.'

'No, it isn't, Sara. He is an angry man, I would say that.'

'And lacking in friends, mistress.'

'He has many friends in the fields.'

'Hah! Those who set themselves to the plough, he speaks for those folk – when no one else does. Burn down *their* houses and no one much minds; but touch one of the bishop's deer ...'

'You speak much like him, Sara.'

'Them that rarely rest,' she says, 'who cannot afford to rest - it is they who are his friends, mistress; those stretched and busy in their planting and sowing, those on the edge of life ... while the greedy lords with their sharp knives pay foul-mouthed jesters to sing songs for them at supper.' I have not heard Sara speak like this. She could be his mother. 'This is not a good land for the beggar, mistress.'

'Though not all beggars are true, Sara.' This does need to be said. 'There are those who pretend for their money, duping the innocent, this is so. I have often walked past them in the morning, with their begging bowl and tears - only later to find them fighting over beer, and snoring in the street, too soaked to go home.'

'So they pretend for their income - but do not the friars do the same?'

'Well ...'

'The friars preach only for their bellies, this is something you know, mistress; they find in scripture whatever suits them, whatever they want to find. They make income from rich men's confessions and poor men's fear, charging folk for a good conscience - a profitable living indeed.'

'I believe Mr Curtgate is an honourable vicar.'

'Then he would be a first; but who knows, perhaps he is?'

'He brought me a cat.'

'He probably stole it from the poor.'

'I don't believe he stole it.'

'Most of the priests claim poverty, that's all I say. They claim they have no money since the plague, since their benefactors died. They beat on the bishop's door, '"as destitute as beggars"' they say, wanting only a '"London home, my Lord – a London home would help so much."' She mimics their subservience. 'They all want a London home where there is more money to be made in the mass.'

'Then I hope the bishop speaks firmly with them.'

'The bishops ain't there, mistress, too busy with the king ... or a fight in France. Wherever the king is, that's where they are, bowing and scraping, crossing themselves and angling for position, to be stewards of his money, to keep the royal accounts and handle his payments ... from their fine London manors.'

'I have not heard you speak like this, Sara. You sound like Mr Ball.'

I am shocked, my breathing is shallow.

'I merely say why Mr Ball will not find many friends, mistress; not in this land.'

'I understand.'

I say this, and I do understand her speech; but I do not understand Sara and where this talk arises in her, gushing out like dirty water from a gutter in a storm.

'Mr Ball is not like the other priests. They take away his church because he forgets to think of himself and his money pouch from morning to dusk! And because his supper plate is wood and not silver!'

'And do you think of me in the same manner, Sara?'

'You, mistress?'

She is surprised.

'Do you think of me as one who cannot be a friend of Mr Ball?' She does not answer me immediately and I fear the truth of my words.

'The anchorites and hermits,' she says, 'they give their lives to prayer and penance, and maybe some are kind, I would not know. I do not judge you for your way of life, mistress.'

This sounds precisely like a judgement.

'I live off your labour, Sara and you appear to hate such people, those of the middle class.'

I do not wish her to hate me.

'I do not warm to pretence, mistress – whatever the class ... nor to the demon who declares himself an angel. No one should speak of God, while chasing gold or reputation. They stand in the shadow of their sin.'

'I just hope ...'

'You cannot speak of God and chase these things. And you do not chase these things, mistress, I do not believe so. A liking for dried herring is not the same.'

Sara laughs and I try.

'But you bring me food and take my waste, my filth ... why?'

Sara breathes in; I hear her breathe.

'Because I have a liking for you, mistress. Is that so strange?'

'And a liking for my calling?'

'I do not serve your calling, Julian, I serve you. You have always been a good girl. Remember how we have known each other ... and I know you to have a good heart and a smile like the sun.'

These words are like warm oil on my soul.

'You always make me smile, Sara.'

'I could not live in a cave such as this, though, I know that much.'

'God is my help.'

'If you say so ... though I help you too; and the poor of this neighbourhood also.'

I feel stupid again.

'Of course, of course, Sara, I am indebted to you, to you all.'

I feel her anger, though with whom, I am unsure. And here I pause, I cannot write anymore, for rather than settling my soul, she stirs it ... just as Mr Ball stirs it.

I wonder if I am vile or useless and if any goodness lies in me. And I fear the path I might take.

13

━━◄►━━

'D o you eat wisely?' she asks.

My straightener looks at me.

'I believe so, Sister Lucy.'

She pauses.

'Abbess.' She says this in a flat manner, without expression. 'Abbess Lucy.'

'Abbess?' She nods. 'You are now abbess at Carrow Abbey?'

'In the grace of God, I am so; and it matters not, not at all, I do not alter ... but it is best you know.'

'And Abbess Hilda?'

'Abbess Hilda died ... and I was chosen.'

'They chose wisely.'

'They chose without choice. They chose me because I live, when so many sisters do not. I am chosen for the virtue of breathing.'

I do not believe this, for Sister Lucy.

'You will make a fine abbess!' I say, and then a thought enters my mind. Has she come to say good-bye? 'But now I wonder. Perhaps, with new responsibilities, you are too busy to attend to my needs?

I would understand. I mean, do you come to say goodbye?'

Her eyebrow is raised, as if I misbehave.

'Would you like that, Julian?'

'No, no!'

'Would you like someone who asked more gentle questions of you?'

'Not at all! That was not my ...'

And she asks the question again. 'So do you eat wisely, Julian?'

'Why do you ask?' I will be frank – I do not like this question.

'You do not look well, girl. You are gaunt.'

'Perhaps I sicken a little ...'

'It is quite clear you do not eat, Julian.'

'I do eat.'

'And so I consider why.' She ignores my words. 'I know there is shame inside you, which can be turned on your body. Is that your way? Shame acts in this manner. Is this the burden you carry?'

'I do not understand ... Abbess.'

'I believe you do.'

'I seek only to love God.'

'But shame bedevils your seeking, it always has. Think, Julian ... and I speak kindly, believe me. But why else would a child ask for an illness unto death, as you did? Do you imagine this to be a normal request?'

'I was perhaps younger, less wise.'

'But the child births the adult. You have in you the tendency to extremes, a tendency to the punishment of self .... which is why I ask if you eat.'

'I do eat.' I say it again.

She shakes her head and smiles.

'You perhaps have not changed as much as you presume from your younger days. Doesn't our Lord deserve the truth?'

'Of course our Lord deserves the truth. And I do eat less – but I eat less because Norwich eats less. Is that so wrong?' I feel the strength of my cause. 'These are austere times and the people of Norwich eat less every week. I know well how people hunger. And why should I have more? Why should I not join them in their suffering?'

'You eat less because of your shame, Julian.' She says this as though she is quite sure. 'You hear the stories from Europe; stories of women hurting their bodies, anorexia mirabilis ... Marvellous Fasting they call it.'

I know of these things; but have honestly thought myself beyond them ... though there is something to admire in their behaviour.

'They say that Catherine of Sienna lives only on the Eucharist,' I tell her.

'Catherine will die, everyone knows it.' Abbess Lucy is cold in manner. 'She will not survive her insistent starvation. She may as well throw herself from a cliff. Do you wish death, Julian?'

I find her question harsh and wish her to leave.

'I try to love the Lord, as do you ... as do the women of Europe.'

'And self-starvation is love?'

'Yes, like Mary at the cross - '

'Mary did not choose the cross, Julian - it was given to her. She did not choose the path of suffering ... suffering was placed in her path. But these women, they choose it - they choose not to eat, to starve their bodies. They cease their woman's cycle but bleed instead from nose and mouth. Is this love for the Lord? Does this give our Lord delight – to see women bleeding so and wasting away?'

Kind Sister Lucy of old has grown into a fiend, this is my thought.

'Some say it makes saints of them.'

'And what do you say, Julian?'

'I do not know.'

'They make crowns of thorns and drive nails into their flesh; they stand for many hours with extended arms. Do you do this?'

'I did it as a child.'

'And the trances given to them in these starved states are reckoned divine visitations - as if God arrives only in pain!'

'Did not Jesus fast for forty days?'

I will not have her speak to me in this severe manner; and so I remind her of this.

'And what of his other days?' she says, leaning forward. 'He fasted for forty but what of the others? Did he not eat happily then? You choose a moment - and make of it his life.'

'You seem much troubled by this, Abbess.'

She draws back.

'I wish only to save you, child, from your shameful desire for punishment.'

'There are rumours of healing among these women – of levitation and floating over walls. I have heard these ...'

'Julian, you must listen! Listen to your substance ... to your substantial self.'

'But surely – am I so wrong, Lucy? – surely we are called to escape our bodies, to escape this imprisonment of the flesh? Are we not bidden by St Paul to control our sensual needs, which so ensnare us?'

The abbess pauses, and takes a deep breath. She looks down into her lap and then looks up smiles.

'God has given you your body, Julian. It is a good body ... I am told even the bishop admired it.'

'I have no interest in ...'

'And your body is the house for His spirit. It is God's house. We look after the house; we care for it, until, in time, it withers with illness or age ... which comes soon enough.' She looks at me, as if to ask if I understand. 'Believe me, Julian – and you know this most cruelly - we meet with suffering along the way, quite enough suffering, without our creating it.'

When Abbess Lucy is gone, I feel faint and exhausted, as if I have been pummelled by hard hands. I pace a little, and then sit by the altar and think ... though my mind cannot settle. And I do know that, when young, such thoughts as these had prevailed. I try not to remember, but I do. I believed then that I must suffer all the dreads, the tempest of fiends and all manner of other pains - otherwise how could I say I loved my saviour? And yes, only in this manner would I be free of my shame.

And I had imagined those days behind me ... but now I wonder.

I drink a little ale and some barley broth. Abbess Lucy has told me to eat, and I do so, in obedience rather than desire ... though I feel God's pleasure in this food. And can it be? Can it be that God is in our sensuality as well as our substance? In both pleasure and pain; in both body and soul? Perhaps this is what Mr Ball says. And that far from being separate, body and spirit render mutual aid, helping each other ... body helping spirit, spirit helping body, until the day our stature is complete in God's kindness?

I feel God's pleasure in my barley broth tonight.

14

My soul is quite unworthy; I return to this sense as I take up the quill again. It will not go away.

I am like the false beggars I spoke of to Sara, pretending something - pretending poverty or pretending prayer, it matters not. So superior on my arrival in this place, I now see I was not good enough to enter.

And when the soul is tempted in some manner, or isolated by distress, then it is the time to pray, this I believe; to make oneself pliable and submissive towards God, this is my truth. But I cannot pray; or not as I would wish to pray. I cannot pray with the feelings of love that are due to our Lord, for I am alone, this is my sense. I belong neither on earth nor in heaven, a mere burden to others ... quite apart from their suffering, hiding away in my cell.

So what do I write?

I write what I know, that sin enfeebles the soul; that sin makes the soul as a bird in the cold, alone in its hunger and weakness; and there is sin in isolation. Did not Adam hide in the garden, fearful to show his face to the Lord? And am I not the same?

I talk with Peter, and perhaps he is an angel; I believe he listens, I must hope so ... though he sleeps a great deal and kills with fierce teeth and claws. But on occasion, he leaps up onto the Christ window and I open the curtain for him to enter the church. He needs to be there, it seems ... so perhaps God is in him, as he is in me. God is nearer to us than our own soul, I hold onto this; and in falling and rising we are preciously kept in the one love. And so it is through scripture, through the Mass and my cat that I learn - love is unalterable, this I know.

And yet this I do not know; or not in my senses. I speak of love without sense, which makes my words like a cloth in the wind, silly and uncertain.

I confess that when I was ill, I had a great longing to be delivered from this world and this life. Such was my suffering, the desire for its end so strong ... I desired only death and to be with my Lord. There are times when this life pinches with both harsh and bitter fingers and to be free from its grip is my only wish.

Though perhaps this is selfish, I do not know. I feel selfish - as one who falls and fails in this manner ... while Mr Ball gains strength from the suffering around him. He seems to ride it, as one who straddles a wild horse, regardless of danger and quite without fear. He seems so much better than I.

So what of God's promise - God's promise to me as I lay on my sick bed, in wondrous recovery? What of his promise that I would be taken from my suffering. This was our Lord's promise, that I would have no kind of suffering, he made this quite clear - no kind of sickness, no manner of displeasure, no unfulfilled desires ... but always joy and bliss without end.

Yet this is not my present path; nor has it been for some while.

And I have kept the wooden boat Richard carved for Lettice; and I have kept the shawl in which Lettice died. I have kept both these things, I could not let them go; but their comfort is ever weaker, like a dying fire, like flames becoming cold.

*

'The mayor wishes to see you,' says Sara, much flattered by the thought, though she hates all talk of mayors.

She arrives earlier than usual. I am kneeling at prayer, remembering our young king and the merchants of the city, who need such petition.

'The mayor?' I ask, and with some surprise and I feel ennobled in some way, that he should come, though he is just a man.

'Perhaps he wishes to contribute; to say thank you on behalf of the city for all your prayers. We do need funds.'

'Is my cost a difficulty, Sara?' I worry about this and do not wish it to be a difficulty. 'I will eat less ...and no herring.'

'Do not concern yourself with nonsense, mistress. Mr Curtgate has the measure of these things ... I just say the support of the mayor would be assistance.'

And then a thought arrives, like a plough through my being; something churns me.

'Do you know the name of our mayor, Sara?'

'I do not know his name,' she says. 'He sent a boy to arrange his visit. He came in the mayor's silk - very grand. A rich yellow and blue, with a gold band. And he comes here!'

'We are not to fret about suffering,' I say, 'not at all.'

'Suffering, mistress? I don't see any suffering in the visit of the mayor, apart from the hypocrisy, falsity and silken puff. I brought it as happy news, news to cheer; for there is quite enough of the other sort.'

'These were the words of God to me in my vision, not to fret - wonderful words, so I speak them.'

'But why all a-fidget now, mistress? I can't understand ...'

'That there is peace beyond the terrors of the mind, Sara; peace between our worried thoughts.'

She is confused and can hardly be blamed for that; she knows not where my mind goes.

'I don't see any terror if the mayor brings money, Julian.'

'Nor do I, Sara, nor do I, no terror at all.' I calm her. And then movement outside the visitor's window; and the veil blows a little in the draft. The visitor sits down. And I hear his breathing, recognise the scent ... and feel faint.

It is Mr Strokelady.

*

I reach for my seat for support, my legs give way, and I sit down, unable to speak.

'Hello, Beatrix,' he says.

The voice chokes me, the sound of it. I struggle to speak.

'My name is Julian.'

'You speak weakly. Are you not well?'

'My name is Julian.'

I speak a little louder.

'Ah, Julian, yes ... Julian, the anchoress of Norwich!' I can hear the awkwardness in his voice. 'You have become quite famous! See - even the mayor comes to your door!'

I do not know why he is here. Nor do I know what to say. Does he seek counsel – or forgiveness? Or is there some other matter?

'Does my mother know you come today?' I ask.

'I do not see so much of your mother now … no. The mayor has much to do, a great deal to do, much to oversee. I know she is sad she does not see you … a great sadness.'

'Why have you come?' I sense his discomfort, amid my own.

'I have wanted to speak with you for a long time.' I stay silent. 'But there is much I have to attend to; with both business and city demanding my time.'

'I am sure you are very busy, Mr Strokelady, you were always … busy; and perhaps too busy to stay here now.'

'No, no …'

'I understand you have much to do.'

God forgive me, I only wish him gone.

'I wish, of course, to support you, Beatrix -'

'My name is Julian.'

'I can hardly call you a boy's name, Beatrix, for you are most certainly a girl!'

'My name is Julian.'

'And that too is sad for your mother, who does her best. A saint some would say. And I have always looked after you, have I not? I hope I have always looked after you. Does the parchment arrive as it should?'

'It does, yes.'

I feel him again, smell him again, hate him again … God forgive me again; hatred arrives at my door, a poisoned word, but the poison is strong inside. And I try to remember the opening of my spiritual eyes, when I

was ill, when the Lord showed me my soul in the middle
of my heart - this he showed me. He showed me Jesus
resting there, at the centre of the soul, in peace and in
rest ... but I only hear screaming now. Does our Lord
scream? He screamed on the cross, nailed and thorned.
But does he now scream for me? The screams may be
mine alone, this is possible; and we must refrain from
the delusion whereby we put into God, what is felt only
in ourselves. My mother would say this; and she is not
always mistaken.

'Why do you come here, Mr Strokelady?' I ask.

'I believe you should call me "Mayor". I am the may-
or of this city.'

'A passing thing - here today but snatched tomorrow.'

'You have not changed!'

'I have changed, Mr Strokelady. I care neither for labels
now ... nor for whitewashed homes or windows of glass.
Perhaps I never did, living my mother's un-well dream.'

He shifts on his stool; I hear him shift.

'Then perhaps you should remember how you took
my money, Beatrix!'

'I do not know what you mean.'

'You seemed happy to take my money then; and I
was most happy you should have it, for I wished only
to help.'

My feelings are difficult to write ... as if he paid to
touch me and I took the payment like a cheese-seller,
handing a slice of myself to him, when it was not so ...
he paid for errands and the like.

'And I come now only to support you; for I am told
you need support in your cell.'

'I do not need support.'

'Sara told me contributions are always helpful in these
difficult times. She says you have received no bequests

from the dying; not so far, at least, which is most regrettable. Do people not remember you as they should, Beatrix?'

I wish Sara had held her tongue.

'My name is Julian. And I have sufficient.'

I feel my neck tighten as I speak; my throat tightens, as though something is forced there, and I find I cannot speak the words I wish to speak, while a vileness drowns me; though I know that when vileness is removed, God and the soul are one and quite impossible to part.

'Then perhaps you wish to say "thank you" to me,' he says and I wonder on his meaning, feeling only confusion: for how am I to thank him? I look across at Peter, who lies by the empty fire, embers smoking in the grate. Stretched there in lazing unconcern, Peter calms me. I like his unconcern.

'As I say 'thank you' to you, Beatrix, no harm ever meant ... you must understand that. And we shall be friends differently now, I as mayor and you ... as you are, past friends in one manner and present friends in another! That is surely our way now? That we be friends.'

'I do not think we were friends, Mr Strokelady; my body does not tell me so.'

It is as though a wild river runs through me.

'You were often my little visitor, Beatrix, and I hope a happy one; I always believed this.'

'I visited your house because my mother wished it ... and now you must go.'

'I will support you, despite your cold face toward me.'

'You must support all people and harm none, if you will understand my meaning.' He is silent, he breathes heavily.

'There are things not easily - '

'And all shall be well, Mr Strokelady. I have only this to say to you ... that all shall be well and all manner of things shall be well.'

I hear him cough and then slowly he rises from the visitor's chair.

'Well, I will take my leave now, Beatrix ...'

'Julian.'

'Julian, yes ... I will take my leave and be on my way. The mayor never sleeps, not in a city such as this, ten thousand souls they say, ten thousand! Only London is larger, and I know some who have been there, with stories to tell ... but glad of your company this day, yes, and that we have spoken ... and glad that all shall be as you say, that all can be well ... we must hope so.'

He speaks as if to himself, as if searching for a priest and muttering confession on the way. I feel he needs to weep and to scream - though perhaps I imagine this, I do not know. But I cannot reach through the curtain, I cannot touch him, my body will not allow and on hearing him leave, I sit for awhile, short of breath, and consider my final words. I am surprised by them and concerned they were offered too cheaply, as if to please him, as if I begged now for his money ... or his parchment.

And I do wonder at the nature of the truth I have offered; and whether it be right to say to this man – to a man such as this - that all shall be well? Can all be well for his sort?

I rise from my stool and lie down by the altar, enjoying the cold stone through the rushes. Peter raises his head, noting my new placement, a little surprised ... and then he lays it down again, fur on stone, his eyes closing in peace.

But my own eyes are open, for I do not know the answer ... the Lord has not granted me to know why sin came into the world and why it forces its way onto girls and becomes so rich and then mayor of this town.

15

Sara has not been for three days and I hunger. I am now without food or word of events around me. I have a little water.

And events have been harsh, like the lashing received by our Lord; harsh unto the spilling of blood and men shouting in the church and the desperate story of Mr Ball.

I have not written on this parchment for some while. I have begun other writing; I write of the revelations granted to me. I try to make sense of them, avoiding delusion ... I have no wish for delusion. They were many years ago now, delivered to me on my death bed. But faith keeps them safe, by the grace of the Holy Spirit, and even now, a ghostly understanding grows in me, an explanation for all that has been, is and will be ... the key to all Christian experience.

I call these visions *The Revelations of Divine Love*, I write on other parchment, and maybe one day they will be read - I hope they will be read, though who can say? In such times as these, nothing is certain, with shouts and burning round about me. And since the noise and violence began, I have not seen Sara and wonder if harm has been done to her.

Sara has told me of uprisings in the county of Kent. 'The noble rebels', this is how she speaks of them; and these people are Sara's friends I discover. She has told me of their journey to London, our capital city, 30,000 marching for 'the people's cause' – the people's cause? What is that?! And who heard of such a thing? They demand the end of the poll tax, talking with the young King Richard – a boy of sixteen years. And then while they talk with the king, some complainants extend their reach, they enter the city with angry hearts.

The archbishop, the king's treasurer and the tax commissioner are all found hiding in the big Tower, whereupon they are dragged out and executed, their heads placed on poles and paraded through the streets of cheering Londoners.

These things I cannot imagine. Such lordly folk killed by farmers! Such terrible darkness! Who has heard of such things? And then the peasants sent home with promises from the young king. He told them that all would be healed and their demands well heard.

'But they were not well heard,' says Sara, 'or perhaps too well heard! For the king's army came, marching in lines with vengeance in their hearts and the killings began, five hundred at the battle of Billericay – how can country folk fight soldiers?' And many others chased, taken from their homes, Sara says, dragged and hanged in their villages. 'Serfs you are and serfs you will remain!' says the king.

'He said those things?'

'Of course he did.'

'But he promised them better.'

Sara laughs with scorn, as though I am an idiot.

'Only a fool trusts the good faith of their rulers; for when, in truth, did the rich ever make things better for the poor?'

'And Mr Ball?' I ask.

I am concerned for Mr Ball.

'John was always a brave young man,' says Sara.

'Was he with the peasants?'

'Of course he was with the peasants. Where else would the man be?' she says ... but I have not seen her since, she has not come, and now there is noise around me - noise in the church, shouts of violence, I do not know what occurs, this quill must stop.

Do they come for me?

*

The violence is close.

I look through the Christ window, I pull back the curtain on the church ... I cannot believe this: men armed with clubs, swords and harsh words, they roughly open doors and grab a woman in a pew by the hair - they do this. She is praying and they grab her by the hair and push her roughly down the aisle.

'Be gone before we put you in the stocks!' they shout.

I take this in, and suddenly the bishop is before me. He reaches in and pulls back the curtain and now stares at me, his face large in the Christ window. I do not recognise him at first; he is no Christ, but wears mail armour and carries a sword.

'We look for rebels, sister!' I cannot speak, I step back. 'We drag them from their homes! We drag them from their sanctuaries! You don't have any in there, do you?'

'There is none here but myself, your Grace.'

He looks through me and looks behind me.

'Calls himself "King of the common rebels".'

'Who, my Lord?'

I do not know who he speaks of.

'Geoffrey fucking Litster, some misconceived dyer of cloth.' The bishop's face almost explodes. 'Took the castle with some rabble, burned the records of finance - and imagines all are now free from debt! But his debt has just begun, believe me! And his head has not half an hour more on his neck - a dyer who will die! So if I discover you hide anyone ...'

'I do not hide anyone.'

Why do I say this? He accuses in rage not insight, and now his face comes nearer to mine, gleaming with sweat and violence; though once this face said prayers.

'Are you a rebel, sister - a quiet and secret rebel? Is Mother Church not enough for you, a wader in the Lollardy shit?'

'I am an obedient child of the church, my Lord.'

I do not wish him to pull down my wall, really I do not; but one word from his sneering mouth and all could be made rubble.

'I hear John Ball was here.'

My heart jerks.

'John Ball?'

'Don't play the innocent maid.'

'He came, it is true - he came to my window, as many come to my window, it is no secret.'

'He came by night, I am told.'

'People choose their hour; and I turn none away. Grace cannot turn away. But he came for counsel only.'

I wonder what he knows, and who has spoken of the visit. I have nothing to hide, though he makes as if I do. But perhaps Mr Ball's words are best not shared ... though am I to lie, should he ask?

'For counsel?' He laughs aloud. 'How would anyone counsel that shit - when all he knows is to talk? There'd be no room for counsel!'

'He has many words in his body, it is true.'

'And none of them good. So?'

'We spoke of God,' I say, for he waits on my answer; and we did speak of God, it is not false.

'He knows only Satan. And what else?'

'We spoke in private, my Lord.'

'There is no *private* here!'

His head lurches forward again, a furious face, like an angry sow, filling the window. I pause in shock.

'We spoke also of paradise.'

'Paradise? Best you describe it well to him - for he'll not be visiting!'

'Paradise past, when God walked in harmony with Adam and Eve.' I am so angry but the bishop merely grunts. 'We prayed together for such things on earth. I prayed for him as I pray for you.'

He steps back from the window. He tires of me, I can see he tires; and I am glad he tires. I do not want him breaking down my wall. All I wish is for him to be gone.

'I have no food or water, your Grace.'

'No food or water, Julian? Why is this?'

His raging done, he seems concerned.

'My servant Sara has not been to me these past three days. I wonder if she is safe, what with the disturbance ... and the arrests.'

'Your delivery has stopped?'

'Sara has not been; I have no support for my keeping.'

'Sara Heady?'

'Yes.'

'The aunt of John Ball? You do not choose well, Julian, really you do not.'

'I did not know.'

Genuinely, I did not know. Sara is John Ball's aunt? Can this be?

'A Lollardy witch, that's what they say; she's in the castle.'

'I am sure they are mistaken; she has been kind to me and never spoken ill of the church.'

Maybe I lie ... but I lie for the truth.

'Mistaken?' he says. 'The mayor speaks against her.'

The mayor?

'The mayor may have reasons other than the truth,' I say. 'She is a true daughter of the church.'

What will they do to her? What *have* they done to her ... and what is she accused of? I do not know and I cannot ask; and then the bishop is called away. His soldiers demand his attention.

'We have him!' they shout. 'We have the priest!'

The bishop smiles, though not with joy.

'You chase a priest?' I ask.

'Not a true priest, your Mr Curtgate,' says the bishop, 'we know him to be otherwise - such unwise friends you possess.'

'But Mr Curtgate ...'

I do not believe this. I do not believe whatever accusation is made.

'Say nothing on his behalf and you might live, Mistress Julian; I do not wish to see your kind neck on the scaffold. Take him away!' he shouts, turning from the Christ window and disappearing from my sight.

I stumble backwards, half-falling against my writing desk. Peter jumps up, disturbed and then gathered.

'Pray for me, Peter,' I say - as if a cat can pray; but I have no other hope in this world. With my friends taken, and in such a fashion, I feel I have lost my substance; I feel I do not exist. This is my sense in the cell, that I am somehow a mist in summer, nothing more. I cannot pray, I can only breathe and touch the wall, feel the rough stone, hungry for food - hungry for substance in my soul. I lie by the door, no longer a door, now hard stone and earthen bricks ... but the door where I entered. I lie at the door, legs and arms curled like a baby, wishing to return to innocence and to joy.

16

There is a rat beneath the Christ window; I see it as I lie on the ground, hungry. I ache for food and can think of little else. This place is a prison, this life a penance and as the remedy, God wills that we rejoice! For he is our keeper while we are here, our way and our heaven ... though where is heaven now? If this is miraculous fasting, it lacks miracle.

Peter, my guardian, is asleep. Time passes, he is not young now, he slows; he prefers warmth and rest to the hunt and the kill. And the years pass for me too. It is 1381 and last week Sara called out a grey hair which has quietly appeared.

'A wisdom hair,' she said.

I do not concern myself with greying hair or the rat ... though I receive the message he brings. He is my divine office this morning, my meditation on the brevity of our lives: for one such as he will eat my corpse when life has left, as they ate the un-gathered plague bodies ... so quickly on the scene and in such numbers, like a swarm of bees, like a swirling river of fur, feasting.

And maybe my body will soon join them, too starved to proceed.

Though a memory comes to mind from my death bed, a vision given, a story played out before my eyes, where I saw two persons in bodily form. I do not find it hard to remember; it was as real as life.

I see a lord and servant, and a strong bond between the two, with the lord looking upon the servant with great love and sweetness. I watch as the lord sends the servant on an errand, the servant leaping up, for he is eager to do his lord's bidding.

I then see the servant travel a while, before trouble occurs, and he falls into a pit, injuring himself greatly. He lies there in pain, waiting in woe, because he cannot turn back to see his lord.

He fears his lord will be angry for his failure to complete the errand and blame him for his fall. But the lord looks on the scene with a different gaze. He sees the servant hurt while serving him, while doing his best ... and thus quite without blame.

'How could I blame you, dear friend? The apology must be mine!'

And far from punishing him, the Lord wonders how he might recompense his servant for such fright and misery. And so, instead of judging him for his failure, he rewards him with abundance, with the servant's plain tunic replaced by a glorious and colourful gown.

I remember this story as I lie on the ground, as my stomach cries and a rat looks on. 'Reward me, O Lord, reward me with abundance, for I too lie in a pit this day, fallen in your service, wondering if ever I shall rise, weak cords of love holding my heart to yours ... for I too have done my best.'

17

The hangings take place later in the day; they include Mr Litster, who dared take Norwich castle and feast there.

I hear his name called out in The Pit. It is across the road from my cell. I hear the crowd and the shouts and the silence, the groans and the prayers, the defiance, the drop and the screams.

Litster dies bravely, as he lived bravely, though maybe unwisely. Who can say? He shouts his cause and promises a reckoning, before his twisting and stomach-ripped death, I have seen these things; I cannot see now, but I have seen before and imagine well.

How many die this day, I do not know; I feel some terror, as though I am falling toward that place, waiting for my walls to be ripped down. I truly believe they will come for me. I wait for my exposure, for if Sara is a witch, declared so by Mother Church, then am I also a witch? I do not believe so - but a shouting crowd might imagine this and they are close indeed, a grunting mass, close and dangerous around me.

The bell rings, a visitor rushes into the shelter.

'She is taken by them!' says the young girl. It is Elizabeth, I know her voice. She is the daughter of Sara, now grown from the girl I knew and full of fear. 'The Mayor accuses her.'

'Mr Strokelady?'

'You know him - you can talk to him.'

'He will not wish to hear from me.'

'He says she is a Lollard, but what is his meaning? I mean, I know she has a mouth ...'

'I do not know his meaning,' I say ... though I wonder whether it might be against me. Am I to blame for Sara's plight? I blame myself quickly. 'But I do know God's meaning.'

'God's meaning is anger; it is always anger.'

'No, his meaning is love, Elizabeth.'

I feel substance in me as I speak, as if I exist once again, beyond my hungry body.

'I don't see love here.'

'His meaning is love and so you must hold yourself in this knowing; knowing beyond our sight.'

'A long way beyond.'

'For if you know this, you know everything and understanding will arise within you, like the daybreak.'

'My mother may not see the daybreak, Mistress Julian - like those who die out there!'

There are more shouts from the crowd. I hear the accused climb the scaffold steps, I know not their crimes, chains banging on the wood. I do not wish to hear more, I wish to hear none of it - neither the prayers nor the killing, nor the gasping gaping crowd. Why do they watch? I tell Elizabeth that all shall be well, but she is gone and I wish that I were too.

I lie in front of the altar, my face to the ceiling. I wish for nightfall and the city silence ... and time passes.

Hunger returns with darting pains. I do not know what the future holds and whether I will starve, whether Mr Strokelady will ensure this - as if I have done him wrong, when I have done him no wrong. I gaze on the cross, my eyes refuse to let it go, as if I question it, as if my eyes consume it, and in the emptiness of my body, made light without food and spacious – a strange sensation. I feel the love of my crucified Lord, beyond my thoughts of Mr Strokelady. It is a strange feeding, an incoming of love ... I am hungry, yet in a manner, filled.

And this is the knowledge which I most easily lose. I know that God is almighty and has the power to do all things; and that he is all wisdom, and knows *how* to do all things. But that he is all love and is willing to do all things – there I stop and this hinders me.

But I feel the willingness of God within my soul, as I lie before the altar ... as the quartering knife rips open the traitor's stomach outside, the awful scream ...

And then the bell rings. I am not expecting a visitor. I jump up. I feel fear.

Who comes to see me, without warning?

*

'Who are you?'
I am afraid.
'I come under orders, Mistress Julian,' says a voice.
'What manner of orders?'
'I come to bring you food and water.'
'Whose orders are these?'
'Shall I pass them through the window?'
I move round to Sara's window, opening the curtain.

'Through this window, if you please.' He is a young man with a kind face and he hands over a basket of provisions. 'Thank you, thank you.' I place it on the ground, truly grateful, as one visited by an angel, though my hand shakes. 'And will you empty my waste?' I ask, for there is need. 'Will your orders allow that?'

'Certainly, Mistress Julian.'

He says it without delay, as if a charming task is suggested.

'I am not your mistress.'

'It is how you are named in the city, mistress.'

I hand over the chamber pot, which does little service to the air, even the Norwich air. But he takes it without complaint of eye or nose and disappears from view. I feel I recognise him in some manner, though cannot be sure.

I place the basket of provisions beneath the squint and open the food cloth. I hardly dare look, I am too eager; I wish to grab. I there discover bread and cheese - such sweet aroma! It is neatly set before me, and with a little fish beside them, separately held. I melt at the glory of both sight and smell and wonder at such love and kindness. There is no creature made, who can fully grasp how much and how sweetly and how tenderly our maker loves us, I feel this now. It is as though it is Easter in the darkness and fear of my cell. Parishioners sometimes deliver cheese to my window in the Easter season; it is a meal of resurrection and such is this.

The young man is at the window again.

'I am returning the chamber pot,' he says.

He passes it through the window. It has been emptied and swilled with water. I take it with thanks and place it in the corner.

'You must tell me your name,' I say.

'My name?' he says, as if he has never been asked before; as if he has not grown into his name or his being.

'Before you go, you must tell me your name. Angels should have names. Otherwise how can I thank you?'

'My name is Bookman, Mistress Julian. Thomas Bookman.'

'And do I know you, Thomas? I feel I know you, I know your voice.'

He pauses.

'We have met, mistress, though whether you remember or not ... well, I doubt it. I came with the priest when you were ill, long ago, when we imagined you dying. He said you were dying.'

'Ah, yes.'

He was there that night, at the time of my visions!

'We all believed you would die.'

'You were the boy who came with the priest?'

'I held the cross.'

'Then you held a thing of beauty. And I remember you through the eyes of weakness.'

He is awkward in my presence.

'I am glad you live, Mistress Julian.'

'So am I, Thomas, so am I ... though I would also be with my Lord, there are days when I wish this.'

The boy turns serious, looking behind him, before his question.

'And will those who died today, mistress, with the noose around their necks,' – again, he looks around – 'will they be with the Lord?'

He turns his head toward The Pit, now silent. I believe the crowd disperses, the corpses taken away in the death carts – less busy these days, now the plague has gone quiet.

'We cannot describe the path beyond our eyes, Thomas.'

'No, mistress.'

'Though I say this to you: I have never known sweet Jesus to blame ... only to love.'

'They say there are flames waiting those who do wrong.'

'Perhaps they are flames of kindliness ... flames of love and laughter. And I need to meet your father.'

I know of his father.

'Why?'

'I believe he can help me.'

'My father is a drunk, mistress – though decent in his dealings.'

'And he handles manuscripts?'

'He is a skilled creator, mistress. Most skilled! He buys books, makes books and sells books – though I should not say more.'

'What more concerns you? You need have no fear with me.'

Thomas pauses and looks around a third time.

'He is a man who likes books in the language of the English, mistress ... which the church does not like. There is a man called Chaucer –'

'I have heard.'

'He writes poems for the king's court.'

I am so excited I forget the food for a moment, as if Thomas is the answer to every prayer.

'And what other names does your father like?'

I have heard the same of Mr Chaucer. I have heard how he uses characters to tell his stories. I wonder whether to do this myself; whether to turn my visions into stories. It is a new idea and one which irritates my thinking with its appeal, leaving me in frustration. But I believe I must write them as I received them, this is my sense; and so I write of myself, the Holy Mother Mary,

God and Jesus. There need be no other characters in my telling - for what part would they play?

'He likes spiritual works, mistress; like Walter Hilton and Richard Rolle ... oh, and *The Cloud*, of course.'

'*The Cloud*?'

'*The Cloud of Unknowing*' - that is the title ... but the author, he stays secret, he prefers to remain hidden.'

'And so extends the unknowing,' I say.

'And perhaps wisely,' says Thomas. 'He may not like the scaffold for himself.' I smile at his kind wisdom. 'But my father likes to copy that one - *The Cloud*, I mean ...when he's sober. We are to smite upon that thick cloud of unknowing with a sharp dart of longing love.'

'Is that what the secret author says?'

'Those are his words, Mistress Julian.'

'They are wonderful words.'

For was I not doing just this before Thomas arrived? Is that not the clearest description of my recent ache for God? A sharp dart of longing love fired at a thick cloud of unknowing?

'And there are other writers, more secret still; but keen to use the new press to spread their thoughts.'

'I would like to read such works, Thomas.'

'You best not read them, mistress.' He frowns at the thought and nods towards the scaffold. 'The church believes all who write in English are Lollards.'

'Thomas ...'

'This is what my father says! It is not so, really it is not – my father is no Lollard, you must know that.'

'I could find payment.'

I wish to read, it will help me; it will help me glimpse the ways of others, help me to write, this is my sense. We had one book in my home when I was a child, some recipes in Latin for the boiling of fruit; though my mother could not read. Mr Strokelady said he had twenty-two books, more than anyone else in Norwich, and he promised to show them to me if I was good; he knew I wished to see them.

'I must go,' says Thomas.

'You do not have to go.'

'I have stayed too long.' He is suddenly nervous.

'Will you return, Thomas?' I like the boy, but I speak to empty space; my angel has left as silently as he arrived and in haste.

But who so thought of me to send this food?

18

The scaffold is gone, the shouts have quietened, stillness returns ... but I am low in spirit.

I have eaten a little, though my stomach is not sated. And I find myself envious of Mr Chaucer who writes for the king's court ... when I write for no one. I write in secret, I write words that can never be shared, words that must be hidden, when he writes freely and to much applause? I imagine this and think his shoes good shoes to be in. And then I wonder whether words are nothing but vanity, both his words and mine?

I do not starve myself these days. Neither do I wear a metal crown at night; nor scourge myself with harsh and bitter thongs, like the nuns in Carrow Abbey before the altar in their cells. As Abbess Lucy said, suffering arrives without our choosing; life is difficult though also beautiful.

I do not judge such fellow Christians; they must do as they do. I know only that I find myself close to the agonies of Christ without such toys and games; and never more so than these last few days when, without company or food, I succumbed to loneliness and desolation.

I once imagined myself above such things; as if I was one more favoured by God. Did I not suggest as much to Mr Curtgate when he warned me, before I entered this enclosure? I hear myself now in shame; I was as haughty with him as a sergeant-at-arms training farm boys.

'God is quite enough for me!' I declared. Yet now? Now I buckle, like a cart in the mud, broke in a ditch.

I weep at my spiritual pride that could not receive his warning. And I do not know where they have taken him. I heard him dragged from the vestry, but have heard nowt since; and there is no one to ask. I sit in my cell, while around me, there is violence in Norwich - a place of retribution for the London march, it seems.

I must send a message to the bishop. I must tell him that Mr Curtgate is no Lollard; how he faithfully offers the mass each week and is troubled by Mr Wyclif ... that I could truthfully say.

I write these things down. But in my cell, I have none to deliver my letter, and so I wait in frustration. I would like to leave this place and myself carry the letter to the bishop's palace. I would ask for an audience, I would speak up.

But I cannot do this, for my life is walled in, my help is walled in. I cannot help Mr Curtgate; and I cannot help Sara.

We do not know what lies ahead, this is the truth; and we mistake our luck for strength. And I wonder again, always the question returns: was it right? Was it right to enter this cell and so remove myself from the world? It seemed an easy choice in that moment, my only choice. I knew it then to be right. But now? Now there seems nothing right about it; and my choice laughs at me ... it mocks me. I cannot even deliver a letter! And who notices me here? And how can I have been so foolish? I have made such problems for myself, there is none other to blame.

And if our substance is love – and this I still believe - then my substance has withered; now a husk in a dry wind. I have known love, and glimpse it sometimes in the hidden corners of my cell; only to lose it, like one abandoned ... abandoned by all that is good.

'My God, my God, why have you forsaken me?' I hear and know the cry of sweet Jesus on the cross and crawl inside his wounds. 'And where is Mr Curtgate?'

And then the voice at my window.

*

'Are you all right, Mistress Julian? You don't look so well.'

It is the voice of Sara; I am quite overwhelmed.

'Sara?'

'Has anyone fed you?'

'I received a basket some days ago ... it has been enough.'

'Sent by who?'

'I do not know ...and I do not care, Sara. To see you safe is enough!'

'Sent by the bishop, do you think?'

'The food? I do not know who sent it and really, it matters not. It matters only that you are well. Elizabeth said ...'

'She came?'

'She came.'

'She shouldn't have.'

'She was worried.'

I am standing at Sara's window; I have pulled back the curtain, better to see her.

'She should not have come with her mithering, causing you worry, mistress.'

'They accuse you of Lollardy, she said. And your appearance is terrible, Sara.'

'And that's a welcome?'

'What did they do?'

'They did their shouting clumsy worst.'

Sara's face is gaunt, grey-skinned and wearied. These days have aged her, as circumstance can.

'I heard it was the mayor, Mr Strokelady, who spoke against you.'

'He is the arse of a fox; I hope you never meet him again.'

Truly, I wish I had never met him firstly.

'I know Mr Strokelady,' I say.

'Of course you do. He paid you a visit, remember - I haven't forgotten.' She is stirred. 'And what came of that but a waste of time? He left his scent but no money.'

'No, I knew him before.'

'You knew him before? Before what?'

'Before he came here ... before he was mayor.'

'You knew him before he was mayor?'

'Yes, I knew him.'

Do I really need to explain these things? The sin appears mine again.

'How did you know him, mistress?'

'As a child. I mean, he was around our house ... after my father died.'

Sara smiles coldly.

'Chasing after your mother, no doubt? She remains a beauty. And he remains an arse.'

'You did not tell me you were the aunt of John Ball.'

'Just as you did not tell of your acquaintance with Mr Strokelady.'

And with that, she seems to put me in my place. But I cannot repeat how I know him. These things are ... they are not for speaking or surely their poison spreads? And perhaps I invent it, and say more than is true? I was young. I do not accuse him ... I will not do this, though perhaps I do ... my body shouts accusation. At the thought of the mayor, it yells like an apprentice, hit hard across the face.

And anyway, I wish to talk about Sara, rather than this man. She has marks on her wrists, rope marks; I see them as she passes the food basket through the window.

'Why was he here?' she asks.

'He came to talk.'

'And his reason?'

'He has his reasons.'

'Your lack of answer does not frighten away the question, mistress ... merely makes it louder. Why did he come? Why did the mayor visit Julian?'

'I cannot speak of it, Sara.'

'Cannot or will not?'

'I am glad only to see you safe.'

'Did you speak to him of me?'

Suddenly, I see her meaning.

'Of course, I ...'

'Did he come ferreting? Was that why he came, asking you to spill our conversations?'

'No, not at all, Sara ... it was not that way, not in any manner! I did not speak of you, I would never do that. I said only that you brought my food, it is no secret.'

'So why did he come?'

I have not seen Sara so hard before. She is like a stone; like a lawyer in the court house.

'I would go to his house ... when younger.' I do not wish for this telling. 'My mother liked me to go to his house.'

'Your mother? Why did she like you to go to his house?'

'He had glass windows, she liked to hear of about them ... and he told me he had possession of twenty-two books. So when he touched me, my mother did not believe my words.'

'When he touched you?'

I pause to remember.

'"How could a man with glass windows, and a fine collection of books, do harm to a little girl? I hardly think so!" Those were her words.' Sara stares. 'It was sinful that I should suggest it, she said. And perhaps I drew him on, she said, perhaps I drew him on. "It is not good for a girl to seek such attention. Win praise by obedience, Beatrix ... win praise by obedience."'

I believe I mimic my mother, as I speak. Sara is like a statue. She says nothing, and moves not at all, but she stares ... and so I tell her further things, difficult deeds. My need is for her to know, to spill a story held in for so long.

'He is the arse of a fox,' she repeats, when I am done. And I pause here, I am exhausted, my quill is not meant for such revelations. Revelations of divine love, these I will write of!

But where is the love in this?

19

'I am concerned for Mr Ball,' I say when Sara arrives the following day.

I have slept well by the altar. I squeezed beneath it and found myself held safe, pressed by the stone, the rushes beneath me, as one secure in a land of trust. I need only trust for all to be well.

'"The mad priest of Kent,"' she says, dully. 'That's what they call him ... though I never met anyone more gathered.'

'And are you truly his aunt?'

I have too many questions.

'I used to know his sister. They lived in the next door village. A family friend - though ain't seen them for a while.'

'And is he - alive?'

'John?'

'Yes, John ... if I may call him so.'

'He escaped London to Coventry.'

She does not seem glad.

'To where?'

'Coventry. It is a town, though not like Norwich ... small, and no boats.'

'And he is safe there?'

I care not about its size today.

'No one's safe, my dear, not these days; they chase you down like the dogs of hell.' They had chased Sara down; she spoke as one chased, as one weary of the fight. 'And they found him soon enough - perhaps someone told them, a loose tongue.'

She seems to look at me. Is it my tongue she questions?

'But is he safe?'

'The king's men took him to St Albans for trial.'

My heart sinks. I am learning what happens in trials.

'He didn't care,' says Sara. 'He didn't care! He denied nothing, nothing at all – he wasn't one for hiding, John Ball, neither as boy nor man.' I feel accused again ...but stay silent. 'There was no regret or sorrow on his lips, they say. He was proud to stand before them, he said that – proud to stand before them and proud to testify to God's kingdom rather than their own: 'To the end of masters and the end of tithes! To paradise reclaimed!"

Sara speaks as though they are her words, released through Mr Ball.

'If he feels fear, he does not show it,' I say, in awe. I know fear in every bone of my body.

'They killed him,' says Sara, and my heart stops. 'Killed him in St Albans.' I am so shocked by these words, they arrive like a blow. 'They gave him a two-day reprieve, mind - a stay of execution.'

'Why?'

'Perhaps they hoped he'd repent of his treason and so save his soul! I wish them luck with that!'

'I don't believe his soul needs saving, Sara.'

'It's their souls that need the saving. Who knows what they did, trying to persuade him to change. But John Ball refused, whatever they did, he refused, and ... he hanged. Hanged, drawn and quartered - let us make it a holy day.'

'A holy day for Mr Ball?'

'Why not?'

'He is no saint for the church, Sara!'

I speak my shock.

'The church would sooner bless a turd, as long as it floats their way. But is he a saint for you, mistress?'

She looks at me. What can I say? He moved me, Mr Ball, he disturbed me; he shamed me in some manner. But a saint, when he speaks only of food, fire and rent? I feel my way as I answer, not knowing my direction.

'I sensed love in the man, Sara, a harsh love, an earthy love ... love I have not seen before. Love released through the things of this earth ... through loaves and fishes, fuel for the fire, clothes for the cold, food for hungry bellies ... as though the poor are the first love of God.'

'Yet not a saint?'

She mocks me, she presses me.

'Everyone is better than me, Sara; this I believe truly.'

'And now he is murdered. Gutted like a pig.'

What am I to say?

'Love is a spreading outwards,' I reply; this sense comes to mind. 'Love is spreading outwards, Sara. And Mr Ball spreads it.'

'And I am to understand that?'

'It has been given to me, this sense.' I know I blush a little and feel foolish, as if I say the wrong thing. 'I mean, I too try to understand, Sara, I too.'

'Then let me take your chamber pot,' she says, 'and I'll do something useful while you try further.'

I have been thinking of Mr Ball, for he is everything I am not. But Sara is too rough with me today, her tone is not warm and her manner, cold; I feel taken apart.

'My meaning, Sara –' I place my hands on the sill of the window, I wish her to listen – 'is that God's kindly love is a spreading outwards ... a spreading outwards in length and breadth, this is my sense; spreading out in height and in depth without end.'

'I don't see much spreading myself.'

'And all love is one love, including the earthy love of Mr Ball.'

'He did what is right and nothing more.' She shrugs her shoulders as she speaks. 'It is simple obedience, we will not drool.'

And I am confused; I know not what Sara wants. I do not know how to please her or what will please her. She praises Mr Ball, she almost swoons over him. Yet then holds back, angry that I praise him. But maybe she likes no flower in the field to grow too high and no remembrance to be too kind ... though her heart is of gold, I know this; and always dutiful towards me.

She has taken my chamber pot. She goes to empty it and I put the basket of food, as I always do, by the altar. I lift the cloth and Peter wakes up, his nose and fading whiskers twitching. There is some ale in a jug, barley broth and some porridge with nuts. I am hungry now, I realise this on smelling the food. I have not had broth for many a day; but I will hold back, I will defer my wants and eat at midday, after the office, this is the better way for my spirit.

My desire now is for silence, for less rage at my window, and for less killing beyond; for I find myself caught in its chatter, scooped up in its fear. Though Sara has not answered my question, I notice this; and when she returns, I ask again.

'Who set you free from your bonds? I saw the rope marks.'

'They had no charge to make. I did not march to London; and they cannot know my thoughts.'

'So why arrest you?'

'And perhaps the bishop wishes you fed, mistress. Perhaps he wishes for your prayers.'

'I wrote to him, on your behalf, Sara; but had no messenger.'

'Then just as well there was no need, my dear. You must never worry for me.'

'Of course, I worry for you. And I spoke for you when they came to the church.'

'They came here?'

'They have taken Mr Curtgate. Did you not know?' She shakes her head slowly. 'The bishop shouted at me through the window; he was loud and disturbed.

'So little change.'

'I told him then of your disappearance. I told him.'

'I must be on my way, mistress.'

'Yes, of course, of course. It is good to see you again, Sara, good to see you ... though I feel I have offended in some way.'

She does not answer and then he arrives, quite without warning. I know the cough. He does not see Sara, who hates him.

And why should she not? And why should I not?

*

'You do not give warning.'

'I bring you a gift, Beatrix.'

'My name is Julian.'

'It is a gift I believe you shall like.'

171

'You must speak with Sara,' I say. 'She looks after my visitors ... now she is freed from unjust imprisonment.'

I say this with purpose.

'I do not know of any imprisonment.' So Mr Stroke-lady claims. 'This city is much troubled, I know that well enough. But this is the mayor who has come to see you - not the shit collector!'

'I see no labels. You are a supplicant, like any other.' I behave as if this is so, though my body tells me otherwise. 'Sara?' I call out, and I go to Sara's window, but she is gone. Is she gone in fury that I speak with this man? It is not my choice.

'You must speak with Sara,' I say.

There is silence. I wonder if he has left.

'Let me at least show you the gift.' He is not gone, and there is nothing I can do. 'It is a book,' he adds. 'Young Thomas told me of your interest, unusual in an anchoress.'

'You know Thomas?'

'I know his drink-soaked father and the printing press he runs. I have purchased several books from there; I am a good customer. And Thomas is a sensible boy ... though one must always watch a printing press.'

He has my interest.

'You bring a book, you say?'

'Ah, a civil tone! Parchment always calms Beatrix!'

'My name is Julian.' We sit in silence again. 'What sort of a book do you bring?' I wonder if this is a trap. If he goes after Sara, perhaps he also comes after me, a cunning hunter, tempting the prey with gorgeous bait. 'I must be careful in my reading, always obedient to Mother Church.'

'We must all be careful in these unsettled times ... Julian. And concerned to hear of your vicar, Mr Curtgate.'

'What have you heard?'

'Only that he was taken and held ... rumours of Lollardy. We drown in rumour in Norwich.'

'Was that also your work?'

I hear him laugh.

'My work? You have too much time to imagine, Beatrix, your cell becomes a box of invention ... when I come only in peace.'

'You do not bring peace.' When did he ever bring peace? 'You cannot even call me by my name.'

'And if you will grant it – if you will - I shall offer this book to you, through the window, and then take my leave. Do you so grant?'

I wish him to leave, certainly ... but I also wish for his book. I pause and I breathe, aware I cannot say no.

'I do so grant,' And I wait. I would dearly love to see this book, to hold this book. And slowly through the curtain it appears ... slowly ... a beautiful leather binding is eased through, passed from one hand to another, from mayor to anchoress. Our hands touch and I wince.

I now hold it; and as I look at the title, I cannot believe that I hold it.

20

'**M**r Curtgate!'
        I am overwhelmed.
        'I wondered if you would like the bread and the wine, Julian? It may have been a while ...'

His face is a shadow through the squint, but his voice clear, though frailer than I recall.

'But Mr Curtgate!'

'It may be that another priest has brought you the mass ... while I have been away.'

He appears to shake a little.

'No, they have not; no one has taken your place ...'

'I thought they might have ...'

'But where have you been? And how do you fare? I saw you taken – well, I heard you taken ...'

'We will not speak of these things, Julian. They are passed.'

'I feared for you, Mr Curtgate. And I prayed for you.' I appear more agitated than he; I believe I have missed him in some manner. 'But you are free?'

'I am released.' He nods.

'And you return as our priest?'

'I do return.'

'I told the bishop you were unstained by Lollardy.'

He pauses.

'I recanted, Julian.'

'You recanted?'

'I saw the sin of my actions; I saw and regretted my heresy. And the bishop graciously smiled on my cause, for which I am most grateful.'

'You saw the sin of which actions?'

'These things are not for us to speak of, Mistress Julian. Now, I must ...'

'But you say there was heresy in you, Mr Curtgate.'

'We must all mind our language, I believe ... in what we say, or indeed write.' Does he speak to me here? 'I realise my error; that is enough for us.'

'Error which you now lay down like a discarded coat?' I need to discover more. 'Are you a Lollard, Mr Curtgate? When you spoke of them to me, did you describe yourself?'

I hear that since the revolt, attitudes have hardened and Mr Wyclif is harassed.

'They call it the Earthquake Synod,' he says, as if it is the doorway to all understanding.

'I do not know what you speak of.'

'The Earthquake Synod. It was a day of much terror in London.'

'What kind of terror?'

In Norwich, we know many different sorts.

'An earthquake, Julian ... during the meeting of the church synod, the earth shook terribly. They say steeples crumbled and large trees fell; that billowing waves rolled up the Thames River overthrowing ships, casting men into the water ... and in the county of Kent, the bell tower of Canterbury Cathedral collapsed.'

'Is this true?'

'All quite true, a most disturbing earthquake ... and terrified priests fled the building.'

'Which building?'

He hurries on without me, like a wild horse. I need to pull him back.

'Where the synod met – the synod which judged Mr Wyclif. They fled in terror, all of them, believing the earthquake to be a warning from God. Like the shepherds on the mountain side - they were filled with much fear.' I am trying to understand. 'But Archbishop Courtney, who had called the synod - he ordered them back to their seats and calmed them. The earthquake, he said, was a natural occurrence, the result of noxious vapours ... vapours which would lose their strength once they burst out of the earth, as Aristotle taught.'

'Do you believe this?'

'And he said that Wyclif's teachings were similar vapours, - and that if they were expelled from the church, its convulsions too would end.'

'So taught by the earthquake, they decided against his learning?'

'The council accepted the archbishop's words, yes. They condemned ten of Mr Wyclif's teachings as heresy; and we in Norwich catch the whirlwind.'

He sounds tired in his spirit. I wonder if he is not exhausted by fear, for fear is most wearing.

'Perhaps God judges the council rather than Mr Wyclif?'

I say this in jest, as if the world is now become a madhouse. I do not know the God of this story.

'Wyclif's followers do say as much. They believe the earthquake comes from God as a judgement on the council. 'They may have condemned Wyclif,' they say, 'but God has condemned them!'

'And you agree, Mr Curtgate? Is this why they took you?'

He sighs.

'I possessed some scriptures in English.'

I am shocked ... but also intrigued.

'Then I would like to read them.'

'You cannot do so.' He is abrupt. 'You must not. It is not possible. '

'I hear the printing presses are busy in Norwich, and that traders bring books from abroad.'

'They are burned,' he says.

'Your scriptures are also burned?'

'Yes, they are. I burned them myself, in the presence of the bishop.'

'You burned them?'

'I placed them on the fire, and held my hand there a moment too long, that I might also feel the pain. The bishop said I should feel pain.' I see the blister on his hand. 'I understand that such books are not helpful.'

'You do?'

'There must be order now, Mistress Julian, or everything will fall. Our nation needs order. The bishop says this. The plague has left the church weak, so many priests dead ... and we will lose the people; while famine makes the city vulnerable, open to riot and looting, which is of the devil. The bishop protects our city, for if we have not order, we have nothing.'

'We have God.'

'But where is God without order?' he asks. 'God cannot be in chaos.'

John Ball comes into my mind, the prophet of chaos. He is alive in my memory, he lives on, I see him, I hear him ... dreaming of a different sort of order. So do I trust the bishop's order? It is the teaching I have received from youth, the truth I have been told, the sure way of things ...

'So it is not wise for anyone to possess such things, Mistress Julian ... there will be burnings.'

'Of books?'

'Of books, certainly ... and of people.'

'People?'

'It will be so, and in our lifetime ... it will be.'

'I do not know how one can burn another.'

'Just be mindful of the times, Julian.'

He hurries away from the window. I close the curtain, my excitement at his return quite melted. But there is another sense in its place.

I know only that I must complete the writing down of my visions. I have pondered them for so long, and written a little. But now they must be lengthened and completed. Life is horrifying and dreadful, yet also sweet and lovely, and it is time I am true to my calling, and speak of loveliness. Whether Mr Curtgate is true to his calling, I do not know; he seems deep in fear. But I cannot pretend that I am here merely to pray. The world collapses around me and I must write what I came here to write.

For now, I put down this testament, and take up my *Revelations of Divine Love,* so help me God.

Part Three

‘You must nought all things that are made, Mr
Strokelady.’

‘Nought all things that are -?’ He almost
bursts. ‘I do not know what you speak of. Really! ...’

I feel his frustration behind the curtain.

And yes, it is many years since I have written here
and many years since I last spoke with this man. Easter
fairs and many prayers have passed, as has Peter, carried out by Sara to I know not where; she never said
and I did not ask.

‘Just leave him with me,’ she said.

And I missed him for a while, particularly at night,
when his strange company soothed me. Peter was a
friendship I had not thought to have.

But I need to explain to Mr Strokelady.

‘In order to know the love of God who is unmade,
you must make as nothing all that is made. Is this not
plain? The unmade cannot enter the made, so we must
unmake our lives, dismantle a little. Do you understand
this, Mr Strokelady?’

He does not understand. How can he understand? I
barely understand myself ... and I do not know why he
has come. He arrived complaining of business; and is
irritable towards the world - a world I cannot change
for him, unless he change himself.

'I think you speak in riddles, Mistress Julian, spiritual riddles, which may play well to monks and hermits who ponder these things ... but perhaps not so well to one such as me.'

'They are not riddles, but clear common sense, Mr Strokelady. I speak to every Christian.'

'It is all Flemish to me, and in an untidy hand.'

Is this so? Have I spent too long with my thoughts, adrift from the world around me? I do not believe so.

'I speak a homely truth, Mr Strokelady - not one distant or obscure. But it is a truth that invites you first to pause. It asks you to pause – and perhaps change - for understanding to arise. And maybe that is its offence ... it asks you to pause and to change.'

He explodes.

'But I cannot do it, woman! I simply can't! I cannot nought all things that are made, and pretend they are not there! How can I do that? I have matters of property and business, affairs of the city. I am not one such as you!'

'And they own your heart?'

'They take my time, for they neither promote nor settle themselves, believe me! Do you wish Norwich to disappear?'

'I wish only for the insubstantial to disappear, and we start with the noughting of self.'

He sighs.

'Can I ask something?'

'You ask can you ask? This is a different way.'

'Did you like the book?'

'The book? Which book?'

I am thrown in my mind. Does he speak of my own writing? He does not know, he cannot know, but I have closed the oven door these past few years and given time to the *Revelations*. I have prayed and written, written and prayed, allowing the visions to find both shape and meaning. I have watched them form, and then form again inside me. I have seen but one visitor a week and heard only the Angelus bell at dusk. I have placed an imaginary circle around myself, to write and then to write again.

And in this way, I have slowed into God.

This is how to find God. To find God you must have calm around you, a stability of life. There can be no knowledge of God in rush and havoc. You must slow ... this is what I would say if somebody inquired. You must close your mind to all that is around you, count it as nought, however it presses. The world and its noise, it fades through lack of attention, I find this. It becomes distant and its shouts less heard. And in this solitude of thought, in this warm cloak of peace, we see beyond this judging world, beyond the oughtery of human guilt, beyond the supposed good and bad, to a silence which is kind, and to a holding, to a love ... to God.

And so the candles have burned; the days and nights have passed; my food has come in and my waste has gone out, and a short version of my visions has become a longer telling.

Am I to tell you this? Yet I wish to tell you, I believe I wish you to know, for *The Revelations of Divine Love* has grown slowly within me. It has baked in the oven of my heart and the solitude of my cell. And yes, much parchment has been burned on the fire - words that do not manage the divine; they are scrumpled in disgust and thrown on the flame. At least my failure warms me!

But yes, in the early days of writing, I would daily read a little of the book delivered by Mr Stroke-lady. It is the book he now asks after: *The Visions of Piers Plowman.* And truly, I wonder at Mr Langland's gift. I read with undimmed excitement, and it became a tyrant, hard to leave, hard to put down, even for prayer.

I have not read such a tale; perhaps its likeness does not exist? It is the story of Will who falls asleep and experiences visions, seeking the truth with the poor Plowman, the dear figure of Christ, as his guide.

We are not the same, Mr Langland and I. He invents his visions, when I do not. I do not believe I could write invention. But, in some manner, his writing carries me, lifts me, draws me to my own story ... and he writes in English, which makes me confident to follow.

'I paid a great deal for it,' says Mr Strokelady.

'And I am most grateful, truly. He is a fine writer.'

'Then I am glad.'

He is quiet for a moment.

'Have you read it?' I ask.

'I have not read it, no.'

'You give it to me - yet you have not read it?'

'I hear enough sermons.'

'But it is not a sermon.'

'Everything is a sermon.'

'It is invention. The writer invents.'

'I do not understand.'

'Mr Langland imagines the story.'

'It is a story?'

I am surprised he does not know this.

'A story imagined by the writer, yes.'

'Can you imagine a story?'

'I believe so.'

'Well, I don't see the point of such invention.' He begins to sound like my father. 'Why would I waste time with another's invention? Perhaps he is not well.'

'I believe our Lord imagined stories, Mr Strokelady ... like the parable of the sower, for instance.'

This seems to halt him.

'I am better with figures than words,' he says, and I wonder if he can read; he probably cannot. 'I just heard Mr Langland speaks of visions, and so I thought ...'

'He does speak of visions.'

'Which I know you also speak of.'

'Indeed ... only I do not imagine mine.' I wish to make this plain. 'They were given to me; they were no invention.'

'And I know from your need of parchment that you must write a great deal.'

'Write?' Do I wish to speak of this? 'Well, yes - I write a little, I suppose.'

'I believe you must write endlessly, Mistress Julian! I see my accounts when the deliveries of parchment are made!'

'I do write, of course I do, I find writing kind to my soul ... I copy St Augustine or perhaps a psalm.'

'Oh?'

'You are surprised?'

'You learned Latin at Carrow? Because as a child, I thought you could not ...'

'I write in English.'

Why should he not know?

'You write in English?' Mr Strokelady chokes a little.

'Why would I not write in English?'

'Well ... it is not the language of the church.'

'I do not write the scriptures, Mr Strokelady.'

'No, no ...'

'But the good folk of Norwich, they sing in English, they chatter in English, they barter in English - when they forget their French - and they weep in English, when pain overwhelms.'

185

'Quite, quite.'

'Mr Chaucer writes in English, Mr Langland writes in English, Mr Rolle writes in English.'

'Yes, well ... but for high-minded matters, for those things pertaining to God and the soul ...'

'Yes?'

What reason will he give?

'Well, it is perhaps a little common?'

Mr Strokelady's father was a blacksmith. He married into wealth from poverty and now, with his tannery and fur business, imagines himself a lord ... and speaks like a close friend of the king.

'I hope it is *very* common, Mr Strokelady - for so is our Lord.'

He is uncomfortable, I hear it.

'The Lollards like English, Julian. You are not one of them, I hope.'

I regret speaking of my writing. But how can I not, when the man gives me parchment, a supply without end?

'In all things I believe as the Holy Church teaches, Mr Strokelady.'

'I'm sure you do, Julian, always a proper little girl.'

There is a silence. I hope I have quieted him. I now wonder if he is angry behind the curtain, or worried. Will he now withdraw his coins for the purchase of parchment?

But I discover his mind is elsewhere.

*

'I do not have long, Mistress Julian.'

He sounds sad.

'Then I will not keep you.'

'No, I mean I do have not many years left to me.'

And in truth, I hear the age in his bones as he speaks. Behind the curtain is not the man I once knew – strong, swaggering and sweet-smelling. Instead, a sagging figure sits there ... a man with grey hair or perhaps no hair; a man with wooden teeth and transparent skin, blotched a little purple ... a man whose life on this earth, the steady gathering of wealth, is behind him.

'You must be careful,' he adds.

'Have no fear for me. I will not be read outside this cell, Mr Strokelady; that is quite certain. After all, the devil laughs when a woman writes - as I believe you once told me.'

'I know more of tanning than books ... a great deal more.' There is sorrow in his voice, perhaps the first I have heard; he is fragile, like a cracked pot. 'Do you believe we can start again?' he asks.

'Start again?'

I have never heard such a question. Most wish only to continue as they are.

'I believe the noughting of ourselves *is* to start again, Mr Strokelady.'

'Can you not call me Adam?'

And can I? Can I call this monster Adam?

'I do not know,' I say.

'And I do not know what this noughting means! Or what else there is a must do! I confess my sins, Mistress Julian.'

'Which sins?'

'And I attend mass!'

'But the wall remains.'

'What wall?'

'The wall remains ... when there is no wall.'

'You best explain; I am quite lost. You do not speak as a priest.'

'The wall between ourselves and God was built by the first Adam ... and you are his heir, in every way, it seems.'

'What wall do you speak of? I have built no wall.'

'A wall built by our worldly business, our worried demands, our anxious seeking ... our hiding in the hedge ... as Adam did in Eden.'

I hear a resigned laugh.

'Perhaps it is God who makes us anxious! And the church which takes our peace! I find no peace in the friars' sermons - that is quite certain! They talk only of hell and fear, which scarcely calms the soul.'

He is stirred with anger; though I also hear a man trapped in an alley, chased by his enemies and nowhere now to run.

And then it occurs.

'I forgive you, Mr Strokelady.' I say these words without plan; they arise unbidden in me. 'I forgive you.'

'You forgive me?' He asks as if this cannot be believed; as a man who cannot believe his enemies quite gone. 'You mean this, Bea – Julian?'

Do I mean this? Do I forgive truly, the mooring ropes cut, the boat released to the sea? And I do.

'I forgive you for past deeds towards myself.'

And so I feel, truly ... a deep letting go, though not of my making. Like the heavy rains, which wash all away in torrent and flood, it is taking my feelings, swilling away my past after all these years ... and none more surprised than I. I could not have imagined this moment; it is like a flooding of the banks, a spilling over. And this is done, not for his sake; it is not balm thrown to please or to ease an old man's woes. Rather, these words are for my sake, the speaking of something within me, that I cannot hold back, an impossible surge.

He is crying, I believe. He sobs behind the curtain, his body jerking.

'That is all I ask, Beatrix.' He can barely speak. He seems to lose his voice. 'That is ... that is all I have ever asked.'

'Everything has a season.' I am still in shock myself, though something true appears, which I speak. 'And perhaps you needed first to be sorry ... rather than guilty.'

'But I am guilty - I have always been guilty!'

'And it blinded you to the sorrow, which is the truer feeling.'

'I cannot bear the sorrow.'

'We can bear all things with God's grace.'

'No, no ...'

'In guilt, the walls between God and ourselves grow higher, built by our terror; but in sorrow, the walls collapse, melted by our tears.'

He is tearful again, and I allow this for a while.

'I will go, I will go ... but I am sorry, I ... I am very, very sorry.'

'So all shall be well, Adam, and all manner of things shall be well ... for between God and ourselves, there is no between.'

'We can start again?'

He sounds like a child with his orange at Christmas.

21

There are rumours. Sara says the market has more rumours than parsnips, and there are many of those.

Mr Bookman's shop is closed down; there was a book burning in the street outside. The new mayor seeks the bishop's eye, and so chases the heretics with his hired men and sergeants-at-arms. I have not seen Thomas; I do not know how his father fares. Neither do I know how Thomas fares. I hope with an ache that my young angel is safe.

And darkening my spirit is the news of Matilda. She was an anchoress at St Peter's, in the county of Leicester. We are told she was dragged forcibly from her cell for sayings considered too learned for a woman. I do not understand the meaning of this and have concerns that this also could be my fate.

'Do not be too wise, Mistress Julian, that's all I say,' says Sara.

I do not know how to answer.

'Too wise?'

'In these present days,' says Sara, 'wisdom in a woman is ill-advised.'

'Then how fortunate I have never been wise in my life!'

I make merry with the idea.

'No jesting, mistress - for here is no jest.'

'So I am to sound stupid, Sara, to stay as Christ called me to be? I am to speak as an ass to please the church?'

Matilda was questioned, Sara tells me. She was questioned by the bishop and sent to a convent to be 'reined in'.

'Reined in?' I ask. 'Like a disturbed horse?'

'She had to learn a different faith, the true faith ... just as you will, unless careful.'

I hoped in my cell to be beyond their reach, and so find safety and peace. But Matilda's story offers no peace.

'John Ball - he would not have agreed to sound stupid to save his life. I do not think he would.'

'We are not all John Ball,' says Sara.

'But we must each protect our gift.'

And I know what I must do ... I know it quite clearly, as if I'd always known; though the thought comes to me only in this moment.

'Sara, you are to find Abbess Lucy and bring her here. Will you do this for me?'

'Abbess Lucy? She is not so young now.'

'I know, I know.'

'If she lives at all.'

'We must hope she lives.'

'They say at Carrow Abbey she does not have long; and that was a winter ago.'

'And maybe I do not have long, Sara, which is why you must bring her.'

'I cannot bring a corpse.'

'But if she lives ...'

'She will not easily make the walk.'

'Then bring her in a cart! Please!'

'You wish to kill her yourself?'

'I wish to see her. I must see her. She is the only one who can help me.'

I see disappointment in Sara's face and feel again the foolishness of my words.

'I mean, you help me always, Sara, of course you do; you save me daily, come wind, rain or ice.'

'I'll leave now, mistress.'

'But in this matter ... well, I would not wish to endanger you, you have been arrested before ...'

But she is gone. I sense her leaving and hear her absence. I believe I have spoken foolishly and upset her.

And will she now take the message?

22

———⟫●⟨———

I give the pages a final wash, to preserve the ink. I use my fingers to spread the white of the egg. The ink is dry and holds its lines beneath the wet of the egg; it sits safe and secure beneath the drying sheen. I work carefully, though in haste. I feel urgency.

I can bind a book myself; I bound many at the abbey. I stitch the pages together, they each become joined - difference made as one. I then secure them between two pieces of the flat wood I brought with me. The wood is Richard's work, now joyfully used after many years.

'You will write a book one day, I believe you will!' he had said. 'Don't know as who will read it, mind.'

And I do not know either; but I believe these words are given to me for a purpose, and I think of him now, as our work becomes one, my words and his binding; and like the pages, we are somehow joined. Dear Richard, my sweetest friend, my love ... I cry, and wipe the tears with my smock ... I need clear eyes today.

I have soft leather from Thomas. I press the leather against the wood, gentle but firm, a sweet joining, with wheat paste for gluing, a little on both the leather and the wood. I press it for a while, and smooth it with my hand, press and smooth, for this is my sweet child, as Lettice was my sweet child ... I will not lose her also.

And then a voice at the visitor's window. I move hastily to cover my work, like a child caught out. I do not expect anyone and nor do I wish for them.

'Mistress Julian?'

'Yes? Who is it? You must wait a moment.'

I place the book beneath the altar and move towards the window.

'I have a visitor for you.'

'I will have no visitors today. You must talk with Sara.'

'Sara has died.'

There is a mistake.

'She cannot have died. I saw her yesterday.'

As if this somehow brings her to life.

'She is dead, Mistress Julian.'

The voice is firm but patient.

'I saw her only yesterday.' I say it again. 'She was well.'

'She has been taken in the night ... by a fever.'

'The plague?'

'We do not know.'

'But if the illness came so quick ...'

'News came to our household only this morning. There is much we still do not know.'

Yet I am hungry for detail.

'And which household do you come from?' I do not recognise this voice; a woman, perhaps not long in her adult years, but clear and firm.

'Your mother's household,' she says.

'My mother's?'

'And she is here.'

'Who is here?'
'You mother. She waits outside.'

*

My body sways a little at the thought of her so close.
I feel a cold blanket thrown over my soul, a dread. We
have not spoken since I entered my cell twenty-five
years ago, and this is a long while. I have wondered if
she still lives; though she told me her funeral was no
longer my concern.

'We will not pretend you care,' she had said and
spoke in anger.

'I cannot see her,' I say to my visitor. 'Not now, not
today.' My mind is a chaos, and disturbance rises up
in my body.

'Well ...'

'I'm sorry, I do not know your name - or to whom
I speak.'

'My name is Philippa'

'God be with you, Philippa ... a rare name.'

Let me at least be kind to the messenger.

'I am named after the queen.'

'Philippa of Hainault – I remember Sara speaking
of her.'

She married our King Edward at the age of fourteen and they remained together for forty-five years.
I had felt a private envy when I heard this ... to have
such time with the one you love, a gift not given to me.

'Though he ran also with that Alice woman towards
the end,' said Sara.

'The king?'

'The king and his busy cock.'

'You mean? ...'

'You know what I mean, mistress. He was poking her.'

This seems so strange.

'But how can a king do such a thing, Sara?'

'That's all kings do - apart from leaning on the poor. And this Alice – she was the queen's Lady-in-Waiting, would you have it? Arranging her bed clothes and bowing all day long! But there was no waiting in the evening when the king called.'

I keep these things to myself, however. I believe we think a great deal more than we say and for good reason.

'I hear she was a fine queen,' I say to Philippa.

'I care little,' she answers. 'The name was my father's choice, not my own. For myself, I do not wish to be another, whether queen or pauper.'

I like her spirit.

'Your substance is quite your own, Philippa, this is clear.'

'And your mother, Mistress Julian - she has taken great trouble to come here to see you.'

I receive these words, and smile; though not in happiness.

'It is the first time she has taken such trouble,' I say, my voice strained.

'She wishes to see you.'

'She has not wished that for these twenty-five years.'

'I believe she has always wished it, mistress – but perhaps been unable ...'

'I cannot see her now, Philippa,' I say, my decision made. 'I think too much of Sara.'

'Yes.'

'I cannot speak how grievous this is to me, this news of her death. It is most grievous.' I need silence in this moment, like a drowning man needs air ... yet I cannot quite say 'No'. 'Perhaps if you leave me for a while ... and then return.'

'This is difficult, mistress ...'

'It must be the way. I will not see her now ... I cannot.'

'We will return at the strike of midday, then.'

'At midday?'

This is but one hour away.

'I do not believe we can wait longer.'

'I understand ... though I wish it were not this day.'

'I believe it would be a kindness, mistress.'

'And I owe her this kindness?'

'She struggles to move; to come this way again ...'

'Then I will see her shortly,' I sigh, 'at the strike of midday. But now let me alone ... and perhaps solitude can draw tears from me, and begin my healing.'

And so they leave and I kneel at the altar and gaze at the cross, wishing to cry ... but I cannot cry. And I find my eyes drawn away from the cross, away from the suffering of my Lord, and turned instead towards Sara's window, where yesterday she stood, where yesterday I saw her, as I had always seen her across the years ... passing food through, receiving my stench and my waste.

'Sara!' It is all I can say.

I think of her holding Lettice, when no life was left in my girl, handing her little body to me ... then going through to see Richard and shouting out 'My God!' She had not been ready for the mess, for the pus and blood staining the bed, the lanced body, blue in death.

Sara and I have lived much together, I cannot believe she will not be here again; and she did not say goodbye.

'Sara!'

*

'So where is love?' I ask this, here in my cell as I wait for my mother.

The only physician here can be love, for only love brings life; it stands closer to God than any other healer. But where is she? Has this good doctor also gone north? Or maybe south, east or west? I feel not her presence now, and have not for a while ... though a hazelnut lies on the ground. I notice it lying still in the rushes. It must have fallen from yesterday's basket, brought by Sara. She brought some nuts saying they were good for the winter.

'Tough little buggers,' she said, 'hardy against the cold.'

Though she spoke more of herself than the nuts.

'We will eat them together,' I'd said ... and so we had, sharing a meal of winter nuts ... a last supper, now I see this ... a last supper of nuts.

But one must have fallen, and I pick it up, not wishing to encourage mice ... and a strange calm arrives, as I hold it in my hand. I sense the greeting of God through this little messenger, as round as a ball – and I know it is all that is made. I know this in my heart. So tiny in my fingers ... yet it lasts, and ever shall last, for God loves it. It is as if this nut, found on my floor, holds all secrets; a vessel of such plenitude, such hope.

So perhaps love has not journeyed north with the fleeing physicians. Perhaps love has stayed, for as my breathing slows, one truth, and then another, and then another still gather round this nut. They take shape in my mind ... or perhaps my heart, I cannot tell; and the first truth is that God made it; the second is that God loves it and the third is that God keeps it. Made ... loved ... kept.

I am quite taken up by these thoughts, like Elijah in the chariot, for here is grace, quite uninvited and unexpected ... and words do no justice to the change within my soul. I lie back and laugh, my head on the rushes, looking upwards from the ground, towards the smoke hole.

I am stilled and quiet and breathe each revelation ... and though the truths shimmer as ghosts, elusive in meaning and vague to touch, they gain strength in me, take form and body, this hazelnut made, loved and kept by God ... and I am of one substance with him, in rest and happiness; that is to say, I am joined to him in this moment, with no created thing between my God and me. Such joy! And the hazelnut is Sara, this I know; and the hazelnut is Mr Ball, Richard and Lettice and the hazelnut is all Christians and the hazelnut is everything that is made ... made, loved and kept ...

And then the cathedral bells strike midday, a rich peal across the city, and as the last chime dies on the Norwich air, the voice speaks at the window.

'Beatrix? Are you there? It's your mother.'

23

Peace dissolves. It is many winters since I spoke with my mother; I do not know where to begin. I hold the hazelnut, I feel it round and smooth in my hand; I take up my position and search for words.

'I am here, mother.' There is silence. 'Are you well?' My throat is tight.

'I shall not come again, that's for certain.'

I hear her wheezing a little, as if this has been great trouble. I sit by the visitor's window, but place myself sideways; I speak across it, so I can see also the altar and the cross; that I may gaze on my Lord.

'Are you comfortable?'

'There is no comfort here. No wonder you don't get many visitors.'

'I believe you are used to a cushion, mother, a softer life.'

'I'm used to a seat that sits well on the floor and does not sway like a boat in a storm.'

'Others have not spoken of this.'

'They probably thought it.'

I breathe deeply.

'And Philippa has brought you?'

'I could hardly come alone.'

'It was kind of her.'

'And then made to wait ... to see my own daughter ... made to wait to see my own daughter!'

She mutters this, so it is hard to hear. I continue to hold the nut, pressing it in my palm ... made, loved and kept. I have never needed it more.

'I am sorry for the wait, mother - but I had no warning of your coming. And received difficult news today ... as you know.'

I find myself a girl again, as if I must explain and apologise.

'Warning? You need warning of your mother?'

'Philippa brought grievous news of Sara.'

'We must all die, Beatrix.'

'I know, mother ... I know that well. But we may also feel.'

'I don't wish for people mourning me - mithering on about their grief; I'll be happier dead.'

I notice my body tightening; I find it hard to breathe.

'I could not see you; not in that moment. I needed ... time.'

'It seems that *she* is your mother!'

'Who?'

'This Sara woman!'

I gaze on the cross, on the tortured figure of Christ, and hear him speaking, as in the gospel, when unready, he too turned his mother away: 'Who is my mother and who are my brothers?' he asked those around him. And pointing to his followers gathered around, he said, 'Here are my mother and my brothers!'

What offence must have been taken at our Lord's words! What outrage caused! That he should speak to his mother in this manner! Yet in this moment, I understand, for only the motherhood and sisterhood of Sara touches my heart.

'All these years she has served me, mother. Through summers and winters, through cold and wet, Sara has brought me my food and taken my waste.' I am angry as I speak, and choke a little. Tears arise. 'She has kept me alive, mother ... and spoken words of support along the way ... never abandoning me, though she had reason enough.'

'I am sure she has been quite perfect!'

'She was loyal.'

I hear her sniff with disdain.

'Others, I'm sure, would have done it, Beatrix. Others would have brought you food. It is not so hard to play the saint, with everyone looking on, admiring your virtue.'

'Yet you, mother - you, I have not seen.'

'Philippa!' My mother calls out.

'Yes?' I hear a distant reply. Philippa waits outside.

'No matter, no matter,' she replies. 'I won't be long.' And then to me: 'I just check that she's OK. She has not been well.'

'You can remain as long as you wish,' calls Philippa. 'As long as you don't get cold.'

'Where did you find her?' I ask.

'Find her? Who, Philippa? Did she not say? I thought you knew.'

'Knew what?'

'She's Mr Strokelady's daughter.'

'Really?' I cannot hide my interest.

'She probably wishes for my house when I die ... and who knows, perhaps she shall receive it, as my own daughter needs it not.'

It is as if I leave my body and see the two of us from above.

'You have a store room of resentment, mother, and it seems stacked high with supplies. As one resentment is consumed, another takes its place, waiting its turn. I cannot help you.'

'You did not leave her as you left me.'

'Who?'

'This Sara woman. You take yourself off, you change your name, you seal yourself away ... did the perfect Sara have to face such things?'

She speaks as one abandoned, thin-skinned to the slight, a victim cruelly cast aside.

'I do not know why you have come, mother. And if you come only to reprimand, then name your offence, speak it all ... and then go.'

I can say no other than this; I feel as one scourged.

'Was I not good enough?' she asks, quieter now.

'I do not know what you mean.'

'That you leave me – for *this*!'

'Children grow and take their leave, this must be so. I do not understand why ...'

'Mr Strokelady said you would be trouble.'

'Mr Strokelady?'

'He always said you were a difficult girl, even when he tried to help you.'

Again, I feel the scourge.

'And you believed him.'

'I certainly did believe him. He became mayor of this city, did he not?'

'With fine glass in his window and a coat of fur. But he had desires way beyond those, mother ... much that was not his to possess.'

'You make no sense.'

'I say only that I would not cling to his judgements.'

'I do not care for this curtain, Beatrix. Can a mother not see her own daughter? Or is the mother found wanting?'

I wish only to see Christ. I am glad of the curtain.

'We are none of us found wanting by God, mother; there is no blame in him for our sin.'

'Oh - I sin, do I?'

'We all sin, mother; but sin is behovely, it is fitting; for his love is around us as a warming coat in the cold; and makes well of our falling.'

'I will not be blamed by you!'

'Our Lord makes both the fall and the rising, so I do not blame you. There is no blame in my words. Why do you say that I ...'

'Everything you say and do blames me in a manner!'

And in this old woman's shout, in her scream, arrives a strange yielding within me - though how can I describe it? I cannot. But her voice is just a voice, and quite without power now to discomfort me. I feel her discomfort, but in myself, know only peace. And I find the change difficult to fathom. Something has dissolved ... or collapsed. I can take no more of what has been. Here is a point of turning, and I stand as one in a shipwreck smashed by the water. I stand in a wreckage of hopes that my mother would become another, kinder soul; and find myself yielding, to earth and to heaven. I yield to mercy, to others, to myself ... to this moment, just as it is.

'I have no blame inside me, mother; you can walk quite free.'

In some glorious exchange of pardon, things are released and things forgiven. I do not need her 'Yes' or her 'No'. Over her part, and her words, I have no control and no need to control. Instead, a quiet yielding to emptiness is my sudden way, like a path in a forest newly discovered, soft under foot ... and light spills like the sun.

I sit in happy shock in my cell, for here is mercy itself. I am pierced by mercy, utter pardon, which frees all faults and makes them void, while my mother asks if I remain? She does not like the quiet.

'I can't see you with this wretched curtain!' she says.

I have no words. Released within me is such space ... a beyond, which is somehow in the middle of things. I hear the voice, it has not changed, and perhaps it never shall; my mother struggles with grace. But I feel no fear, and I feel no judgement, this is the change ... an inscape of complete simplicity and trust.

'I wish you peace, mother,' I say, for it is true; but she does not reply, she is making her way out. I hear her rising with difficulty from the stool, calling for Philippa, saying she can get no sense from me - none at all.

Though I sit in a sense of grace; quite the best of senses.

24

Did Sara speak with Abbess Lucy before she died? It is possible, but weeks have gone by, she has not come and I am ever more concerned. Mr Curtgate tells me we live in troubled times, and looks troubled himself. He says people have disappeared, locked inside gaols where rough things occur; while pulpits spill denunciations of Mr Wyclif and John Ball.

'Never be called a Lollard,' he says to me, 'or they will rip you from here. They will rip you most easily.'

'What another calls me, cannot be my concern,' I say.

'It is very much your concern.'

'I am a simple Christian: what else is there?'

'And a further thing: you must not speak of your writing; not to anyone.'

'I write only for myself, for my devotions.'

'Truly?'

His eyebrows rise, as if he does not believe me. I cannot lie to him. There must be some to whom we do not lie.

'Maybe not only for myself ... who can say?'

'You mean you write for others? You give what you write to others?'

'I do not give it to anyone, and hardly see a crowd of readers gathering. I write because I must write, because God wishes his goodness to be recorded; and he gave me this place in which to work.'

'In which to pray.'

'I pray and I write. The two can hardly be parted.'

'I think some manage it.'

'Well, I cannot.'

'Does the bishop know?'

'He has not asked.'

'He might ask, he asks others – or his sheriffs do, and they are less kind than the bishop.' My face is surprised. 'No, truly.'

'I need Abbess Lucy to come and take my book.' I say it plainly to him, and he is silent for a moment.

'Your *book*? What book?'

I need his help, so I must speak honestly with him. I no longer have Sara by my side, and he has kindly seen to my food these past few weeks, organising folk of the parish to visit every third day.

'I have written a book of the visions I received.'

He is much disturbed.

'You have learned Latin?'

'I have written in English.'

'In *English*?!'

Have I uttered a blasphemy?

'I have written in English - like Mr Hilton and like Mr Rolle, like the author of *The Cloud of Unknowing*.'

'He is wise to stay unknown.'

'Thomas spoke the same.'

'I wish I could be unknown,' he says with a sigh.

'And the same English as Mr Langland and Mr Chaucer.' He nods. 'You know them?' He nods again.

'And that of Mr Wyclif and the Lollards,' he adds, 'who are chased ever more harshly. Mr Wyclif is fortunate to have lordly friends. The rest of us are not so blessed.'

'I need to see Abbess Lucy,' I say. 'Can you help me?' I try to remain calm though Mr Curtgate's words disturb me. 'I will give my book to the abbey, where it can do no harm.'

'It will do you harm if they find it.'

'Then they must not find it. And anyway, they have many books there, I have seen their library, many, many books. Mine will be easily lost.'

'They do not have books written by women in the abbey.'

I do not tell him this is untrue. I do not mention the spiritual writings from Europe that the abbey has silently acquired, including translations of Hildegard of Bingen and the French Beguine Marguerite Porete. He will only remind me that she was burned at the stake in Paris ... and promise me the same.

'My book is very quiet, Mr Curtgate; it will not leap and shout on the shelf.'

'I do not believe you could write a quiet book, Julian.'

'Truly, it whispers ... but it whispers love.'

He mutters something I do not hear.

'Does it have a name, this book?'

'You sound now like an inquisitor.'

'I hope I sound like a friend. We have known each other many years ...'

And this is true, how the years have passed! He married me, did he not? And I do believe I trust him a little, and perhaps much. I must do, to ask such a favour.

'It matters not what it is called.'

'It might matter a great deal.'

The Revelations of Divine Love, I say ... and somehow I grow as I say it. My child has a name, and I speak it for the first time. And it is as if I know it for the first time, as something discreet of myself ... *The Revelations of Divine Love*.

'Is that wise?'

'Is what wise?'

'The name.'

'It is true.'

'But is it wise? The two are not the same.'

I feel his fear again.

'Does not God love us, Mr Curtgate?'

'I will do what I can,' he says, 'concerning the abbess, I mean. But really ... really ...' And then he is gone, muttering again, and I kneel before the altar holding my child, recently named.

And the words of Hildegard come to mind, fresh and luminous, words learned in the scriptorium. They appear in one of her visions and I speak them now, as I have always done, I speak them to myself, to my cell, to the world ... and feel again their magnificence.

'Then I saw a most glorious light. And in this light, the whole of which burned in a most beautiful and shining fire, was the fire of a sapphire man, and that most splendid light poured over the whole of this shining fire, and the shining fire all over the glorious light, and this most excellent light and shining fire cover the whole figure of the man, appearing together as one light in one virtue and power. And I hear this living light say to me: "Behold the meaning of the mysteries of God made plain, that each may discern and understand what this fullness may be, which is without beginning and in which nothing is found lacking.'"

I bless the name of Hildegard.

*

I do not know what is happening, events unravel.

I smell the smoke and hear the surly shouts; and then Thomas arrives at my window, in distress. I know it is Thomas, before he speaks.

'They burn books, mistress, and I must not stay.'

'They burn which books?'

'Wyclif bibles, bibles in English, Lollard writings. I cannot stay - but I did not want you in fearful unknowing. This is a dangerous night and it has come to your door.'

'I see,' I say, much disturbed. 'And your father, Thomas? Are his books in the flames?'

'Some are his books ... beautiful books.'

'And where is he?'

'He is gaoled, mistress, taken away - though we try to have him freed. We tell him not to curse them, and he sobers a little.'

'Do not forget God's love, Thomas.'

'I try not to, mistress.'

'Good boy. It is more real than the flames, truly.'

I speak to myself and the fear rising within.

'Though life is cruel and more difficult than I can say, mistress.'

'It can be darker than dark. Yet you are full of light, Thomas. It shines through the curtain now.'

'Thank you, mistress. I feel it not ... and see it not; but thank you. And you keep safe.' And then in a whisper, 'I speak not of your writing ... not to anyone.'

I scarce hear the words above the crackling fire and the growing crowd, jeering and cheering, though what they cheer, or who they jeer, I know not, gathered round The Pit where the vellum burns and English words melt and curl in the flames.

'Whatever they do to me, I do not speak of it! God be with you, Mistress Julian.'

*

And now arguments start, and another cart arrives, with more books for the flames. The crowd is restless and cold and I wonder if I will have less kindly visitors this night, for despite meaning well, Thomas has not calmed me with his news. My leather-bound child, my careful pages, feels ever more in danger; and I do not know what to do.

I wish for the good sense of Abbess Lucy, but how can she come to me now? She will never get through. And how did I think the abbey might take my child and hide it on their shelves? I have been most foolish.

And then I hear the chant that chills my soul.

'Bring out the witch, bring out the witch!'

I believe some have been at the ale; and whether they speak of me, I do not know. There is laughing and rancour outside, like the night of misrule, when all is turned upside down and darkness reigns.

'Bring out the witch, bring out the witch! She casts a spell on Norwich - and see how we suffer!'

'Calm yourselves, gentlemen, please!' I hear a new voice in the chaos.

'Ooh, "gentlemen", are we?!'

'She is nothing but an anchoress who prays for our souls - in this life and the next! Here is no crime, surely? We ought to be thanking her!'

'It's the Lollard Bookman boy!' one shouts.

'I just saw him talking with the witch!' bawls another.

'What did you tell 'er, Bookman?'

'Or what did you *ask* her? To curse the lot of us?'

I fear now for Thomas.

'I merely tell her what occurs outside her walls. Does she not have a right to know?'

'Then perhaps she has a right to feel the fire as well – to instruct her better about the night!'

I hear a gasp in the crowd, there is noise and scuffle, and feet approaching my cell.

'Put that down!' shouts Thomas. 'Put that ...'But he is drowned by cheers, and now there is noise in the visitor's sanctuary - rough entry, the curtain thrust aside and suddenly through the window is pushed a large burning log, spilling fire and smoke into the cell. I jump back, it lands close to my feet; I turn to see his leering face in the shadows.

'Didn't want you to miss the burning, witch! It'll be you next, you Lollard whore!'

I move away from the window, that I might be private and not exposed. But the log has set fire to the rushes, and thickening smoke fills the cell. I pour water on the burning, and the fire dies, though the rushes smoulder and the wet smoke chokes. I crawl across my cell, fearful for the safety of my child beneath the altar ... I will not lose my child.

Outside, there is the sound of horses.

'What is this?!' a voice bellows.

The crowd goes quiet. It is the bishop, Bishop Henry, who I have no wish to see - though perhaps he saves me.

'And your name?' he asks.

'Roland Drinkwell, your Grace.'

It was Roland at my window; Roland with the burning log.

'And what do you do in the anchoress' cell?'

'They say she's a Lollard witch,'

'A Lollard witch?'

'They say she writes things on parchment, writes curses. So I took some fire to her, believing that is what God will do, your Grace!'

'So you are now God, Drinkwell?'

'No, your Grace -'

He falters a little.

'You blasphemous piece of shit.'

'I seek only ...'

'And blasphemers must feel the devil's flames.'

There is further scuffle and a terrible scream, as I believe Mr Drinkwell is thrown on the fire by the bishop's men. No one should feel those flames. His shriek and pain pierce the night, they pierce me ... though I believe he escapes death and runs into the night.

'See a blasphemer on fire!' shouts the bishop with mockery and great pleasure. 'A hobbling torch lighting Norwich - and hoping for rain! He moves slow but burns well, does he not? Now, more books for the purging fire!'

And so it goes on, and so it goes on.

*

By the tenth hour, I believe the evening is spent. The crowd quietens, as does the fire, exhausted by burning. I imagine the orange heat of the embers, the black leaves of scorched vellum swirling in the night wind. The fire folk go home, glad they are not Drinkwell; and I sit in the charcoal smoke which drifts slowly skywards, the terror in me receding, the invasion over.

But feeling so trapped ... never have I felt so trapped as I feel tonight. I feel like bait tied to a pole. 'Bring out the witch!' they cried and who knows what might have occurred had not the bishop arrived. The terror fades, though; I return to my senses, as my breathing deepens, taking me from the shallow breath of panic. Again, I feel secure in my cell.

And then, at the same window through which the log came, the bishop's face appears.

25

———◦———

'I s this *The Cloud of Unknowing* they speak of?'
    'Your Grace?'
    My voice trembles.
'I cannot see you for smoke!'
He starts laughing. I believe he jests.
'I am here, your Grace.' Grateful for the smog, I
push my child beneath the altar and move towards the
window, where the curtain remains open. I feel naked
without it and exposed. He chokes a little, and pulls
his face back from the opening; but still I see it, and
how strange. I have not seen his face for so many years,
and how old he has become ... how hard and drawn.
    'You pale,' says the bishop, staring at me. 'You're as
pale as the stars, Julian.'
    'Well, I am happy to be as they are, your Grace. I
remember them with joy.'
    'Comes of shutting yourself away from the sun and
the wind - not healthy.'
    'The cross is my sun and the Holy Ghost my wind.'
    'White as a sheet, you are, like a lady of the manor,
spared work in the fields.' He chuckles at the thought.

219

'Mind you, they say Matilda had turned a little grey -
so perhaps they saved her, when they dragged her from
her cell! Saved her from turning grey! It's not natural
- I've always said it's not natural.'

I struggle to speak.

'Whatever my colour, your Grace – and perhaps it is
the smoke - I am grateful for your appearance tonight,
which did me well. I did fear for my unworthy self.'

'We cannot have an anchoress attacked ... unless, of
course, you *are* a Lollard. You're not a Lollard, are you?'

'I am a Christian, your Grace. That is my only name.'

'Drinkwell said you have parchment; that you collect it and write on it.'

'I do not know Mr Drinkwell.'

'But he seems to know of you.'

I note intent in his voice.

'I do not know how - really I do not. He seemed
over-filled with ale to me and speaking ale's nonsense.'

'But is it true what he says, Mistress Julian? Does
the ale also speak with knowledge?'

He is serious. Drinkwell is not his concern. I am
his concern.

'I do not know what he says of me, or what accusation he leaves.'

'He says you have parchment delivered.'

There is impatience in his voice ... and fresh terror
in my soul. I wonder if he can see my child beneath
the altar; and though glad of the smoke, I wish for my
curtain back, to be away from his gaze.

Yet can I lie? He may discover I have parchment,
for secrets do not last long in Norwich. And then what
do I say? Perhaps I will be dragged out of my cell like
Matilda? Perhaps they will search this place? I write
English words for they are the only words I know to

describe my beautiful Lord. Yet the fire outside burns English words - Lollardy words, they say.

I cannot have this man take my child. That is all that I know.

'I pray for you daily, your Grace.'

'I am grateful, Mistress Julian. Pray for true order in this city and a curse on the French.'

'And truly, I am grateful to you.' I do not lie. 'It has been a disturbing night for me; and this burning log might, well – I do not know what would have followed. You come as an angel.'

'Every crowd has its rogues. We'll put him in the stocks tomorrow, let him cool a little ... and the talk of parchment?'

He returns to the parchment, from which I seek to guide him away. It is why he is here. He comes not to bless, but to accuse. And I am at the end of my charm; it can help me no more and I say in my heart, like the drowning St Peter, 'Save me, Lord, save me!'

'Of course, she has parchment, your Grace.'

'Who is that?' says the bishop, leaning forward. He hears a new voice. 'We have company?'

'I ensure she is well supplied,' continues the voice. 'Ink and quills as well.'

It is Abbess Lucy; she stands at Sara's window and my heart leaps. A further angel ... I have so many angels! My visitors cannot see one another; the windows do not face, placed side by side; and my eyes water in the smoke, so that I cannot look easily at either.

'It is Abbess Lucy, your Grace. We seem to visit our friend at a similar hour.'

'A surprising hour for an abbess to be walking the streets.'

'It is only at night that duties do not keep me. I had not expected such, well - activity close by.'

'Heresy burns, that is all. I presume you're glad?'

'I find gladness is a fickle friend, your Grace, coming and going, even on a night such as this. But I'm always glad when our paths meet in the great forest of life. And glad also to be with my child in God, Julian ... though sad she is smitten with fire and smoke. This log is not your work, I trust, Bishop? There has been dark performance here tonight, of that I am sure.'

'You are still Mistress Julian's director?' he asks.

He is vexed to see her, as in equal measure, I delight; for I am at the end of my wits; and the Abbess has all of hers, even in stooping old age. I notice she cannot now hold herself straight of body; it is some years since we have met. Though what will arise with her arrival, I do not know. They speak with each other, and not to me.

'I am, your Grace. I straighten her on occasion.'

'Despite ill-health?'

'We must both transcend age in the cause of God's work, Bishop. I know you stiffen a little these days.'

'I thank God I can still hold a sword and chase Lollards.'

'And frailty can be a channel of God's grace,' continues Lucy, as though the bishop is dumb. 'I find this to be so, as I am sure you do.'

I sense his impatience. The bishop sighs and seems ready to leave.

'And what do you know of parchment, Abbess? You seem well acquainted with the matter.'

'Julian copies for us, your Grace, she always has. She copies for the abbey, her hand improving all the time. One day she might even write well!' I manage a smile as the bishop fidgets. 'She learned her copying skills in our scriptorium, of course, where she loved to work many years ago. I give her a little to do now, for her learning and edification.'

'And what does she copy?'

'She likes St Augustine, your Grace, as I know you do; though I also give her Jerome for balance. And the gospels, of course ... tempered by the firm words of St Paul, lest she slacken.'

'In Latin.'

'In Latin, which she has come to cherish. You must come and inspect her work in our library.'

There is silence for a moment. I am amazed at her words, untruth flowing with such ease. I cannot imagine the bishop will believe it in his heart.

'I wish you good direction, Mistress Julian,' he says. 'And you, Abbess, a safe journey home ... one without incident.'

It sounds like a threat, but I believe he is simply tired. He does not move as once he moved. He rises slowly from the stool, and shuffles in his leaving, his bishop's chain clanking a little on his widening girth, and then lost to sight. I hear him helped onto his horse, lifted up, and carried away into the night, back to the palace where once I stood before him, to ask for this sealing up. And I can hardly remember that young woman; though there must be something of her still, some splinter of the old inside me.

I turn to the abbess who remains. She looks weaker now, suddenly weak, as if her strength left with the bishop, as if no fight remains.

'So what troubles you, my child, that I receive such a desperate plea to come? Mr Curtgate was quite insistent.'

26

They arrive in the morning, a cold calling.

A man-at-arms presents at my window, opening the curtain. He tells me they have come to search my cell. I know him a little, he is called James. I once counselled his mother, who sat where he now stands, and cried until she was empty of tears. He had brought her here and begged me to see her ...he pushed aside the curtain then as well. Though now he tells me he comes to un-brick my cell, and to enter it. He says I am to remain by the altar; that they wish me no harm, and come only for any parchment.

'Mr Drinkwell has been busy,' I say.

'It is the bishop's orders.'

'But Mr Drinkwell's mouth. I do not know the man - but suddenly his word is law.' I sound firm, but inwardly I fall apart at such invasion.

'If you are innocent, Mistress Julian, then where is the concern?' he says.

'Innocent of what? Is parchment now a crime in England?'

'It is the writing on the parchment, mistress, as you know ... not the parchment, but the writing on it.' He speaks other people's words; he is only young. He does what he is told. 'And English is the language of Lollardy.'

'And also of the market place and home, James ... and the language of your mother. It is a more homely way to speak.'

'But if you are innocent ...'

'And if not?'

My mind races ahead; I attempt to call it back. I remember the hazelnut but cannot hold the feeling.

'It is not ours to argue with you, mistress; only to search.'

'I seek no argument, truly. But if you find English words?'

He looks concerned; he wonders what to reveal.

'Then we are to take you to the palace.'

So they have come to remove me, like they did Matilda.

'What would your mother think, James?' He blushes, embarrassed. Perhaps he hoped I had forgotten. 'I am glad we were able to speak ... and I hope she is in health.'

'She is dead, Mistress Julian; but I live and I am not her ... but a man under orders.'

'We must be careful of orders, James. They do not lead always to life. But do what you must do.'

My voice quivers, I feel such ... I do not know what I feel. I feel weak, I feel shock, I feel strong with rage ... I do not know. I cannot imagine this entry. The man disappears from my window, I hear orders given ... and then rough assault on the stones begins. They are shaking loose, dust falling, stones jarred - a terrible assault on my cell takes place, the noise like thunder. This is an attack on myself and my calling! And then the men

themselves, they appear gradually, as if in nightmare
– grunting, hammering on my cell with some batter-
ing pole, until a small opening appears, a hole of light,
I gaze at the light ... and then bending low, amid the
wreckage, they enter.

The two men enter my cell, James and another.

I sit rigid by the altar, though they are ill at ease upon
arrival, too large for the space, trampling on my quiet.

'The bishop gives you fine boots and jerkins for your
work,' I say, as though to build a wall between us. 'Expensive leather. Does that help you forget what you now do?'

They walk past my bucket of waste, look through
the Christ window into the church and then stop at
my writing desk. They pick up the sheet of parchment
there. I do not believe they can read, but they take it.

They look in my food basket and then walk towards me.

'You must move a little, mistress.'

'This is my home.'

'We need to look under the altar,' says James. He
tries to be firm.

'It would be better to kneel before it.'

'So if you can just move away.'

There is nowhere else for them to look. My home
is not a castle with hidden stairs and closets; but I am
stunned by their closeness, men so close, no wall between us, their muddied boots trampling the rushes,
their sweat in my nostrils.

I rise and move aside and James steps forward and
stoops. He peers into the darkness beneath the altar,
and feels around with his hands.

There is nothing there.

*

They leave as they came, with clumsy noise. They take only the piece of parchment they found on the writing desk.

'You will now rebuild the wall,' I say. I feel exposed by its absence; it must be restored. 'You will now rebuild the wall!'

'We will have it right mended, Mistress Julian. It will be done in the morning. But now we must be on our way ... with the parchment.'

'You leave a hole in my cell? You destroy my cell - then walk away?'

'In the morning, mistress, in the morning.'

He wishes to be away from this place, that I can see; though perhaps more than that, he wishes to be away from me. He holds the parchment found, as though it is a mortal sin, a piece of hell, something to justify his wall-breaking. But beneath his airs, I believe he feels the shame – the shame of obedience to orders. His fine apparel, boots and jerkin – he is better clothed than his father by far. These things, they nibble at his soul, like a hungry mouse with cheese.

'The kingdom must be protected,' he adds.

'Protected from you, perhaps.'

'Protected from those who would overthrow it.'

'You have left nothing to overthrow.'

Then they are gone ... but the hole in my wall remains. I am in shock. I stand away from it, as though it is dangerous to me, and might attack, like a wolf. I believe I fear it and the escape it offers. I fear the chance to leave, to stand again beneath the sky. I am overwhelmed, quite suddenly, with the desire to walk in the herb garden, to sniff and gather dill, hyssop, betony and sage. I wish to walk among the foxgloves, planted for the Blessed Virgin Mary and with healing powers. Or gaze again on the rose, the thorny beauty of our Lord's great suffering. I have laughed at Satan ... but feel now that he laughs at me, and invites me out.

'Only a few steps, mistress, and then you can return.'

And I am drawn towards the opening, for in truth, a few steps can hurt no one. And perhaps this is a gift from God, a blessing bestowed after terror. Outside, I can see grass - a green I have forgotten and it startles my eyes. I have forgotten colour. Such rains have fallen of late, the green is bright ... I'm told the roads are an April slush. But I could walk a little on the grass, with no harm done, to give glory to God ... and greet the oak tree that stands beside Richard and Lettice.

Sunlight now spills through the gap, touching the fallen stones and spreading across my floor. It falls like a pale-gold carpet and I kneel to feel its warmth on my neck and hands; I lie down to know its smile on my face. Through the opening I see bluebells, spreading merrily, small trumpets of praise - such wonder I can scarce take in.

'Mistress Julian!'

In surprise, I turn quickly to look up and hurt my neck.

'Thomas?'

Thomas is at Sara's window. He perhaps wonders why I lie on the ground.

'Are you all right? Are you hurt?'

'No, I'm ...'

'I was told men broke down your wall.'

'They were the bishop's men,' I say, rising. 'You are kind to visit.'

'The bishop's men?' And now he is full of fear. 'And what did they look for?'

'They looked for parchment, Thomas.'

'And did they find any?'

'They found the Lord's Prayer, written in Latin.'

'In Latin?'

'I can write the Lord's prayer in Latin. I know it well enough from the scriptorium. Indeed, the bishop may be reading it now, and may God bless him in his study.'

'And was anything else ... discovered?'

'I do not know what you mean, Thomas.'

I smile and some relief spreads across his young face.

'We will have the wall mended this very day, Mistress Julian, if that is your wish.'

'I am grateful, Thomas.'

He is a good boy, ever attentive to my needs; though no one comes in the afternoon; or in the evening. The wall-menders are busy, no doubt; labourers in need of their pay, and with many walls to mend. And perhaps Thomas is better at making a book than healing battered stones; the world is differently skilled.

And so as evening falls, and the light fades, the hole remains; as my night candle burns, as I read the office, as I listen to the bell strike the ninth hour, the hole remains; as I contemplate Mrs Wagstaffe who came today with a bag of troubles, as all proceeds quite as normal ... the hole remains. I pray for the afflicted and oppressed, for sinners, orphans and widows, for those in peril on the sea, for the dying and for all those who mourn their loss, for the soul of Sara, for the soul of John Ball ... and then without thought, I rise from my seat, stoop low at the broken entrance of my cell – beaten open by the bishop's men - step over the stones and ease myself from my anchorhold.

I step outside into the night air and the star-lit dark.

*

The grass is cold and wet on my feet. It is almost too much; such awakening of feeling! And then looking up, the vast black sky overhead and frightening in size, I stagger a little, unprepared. I am caught in the light of the creamy moon, near bright as the sun, and a myriad of stars. So many? I do not remember so many or the heavens so large and so close, truly I do not, and I tumble and whirl in my head. I become unsteady on my feet, my balance quite gone. I fear I will be lost in this expanse, consumed by magnificence. And I am caught up in the words of the eighth psalm.

When I ponder your heavens, the work of your hands, the moon and the stars, which you have set in place: what is mankind that you are mindful of them, or human souls that you care for them?

You have made them barely lower than the angels and crowned them with such glory and honour.

I kneel down, holding on for dear life - like a child too far up a tree, grabbing at a branch to bring calm.

Though beyond wonder is terror. I am as one who has trespassed on another's land and now fears the hunting dogs. This world is too large, too wonderful, too dangerous for my senses to manage; the shadowy trees loom over me, swaying as though alive; and the soft-scented flowers, so swift to my senses, like strong wine. Such trepidation in my soul, such un-boundaried delight ... I am laughing on the ground, not caring if another hears.

And now slowly, I stand. But I am careful and deliberate in my rising - as a seaman steadying himself on a rolling ship, lifted and shifted by the waves. I sense the oak tree close by. It draws me to itself. I walk slowly towards it and reach out to touch the bark. It is rough on my fingers. I feel its life and strength through my palms, the pulse of its heart, the presence of God in the wood. I turn and lean myself against it. I lean in, like a child against her father, knowing herself secure and safe, knowing herself made, loved and kept. Tears arise in me, though whether in sadness or hope, I cannot tell, and maybe they tell of both. For the years roll away, and I am small again ... so small.

The chill wind on my face, brushing me with its life ... I have never been better stroked. And I understand with sureness, with absolute certainness, that it is both easier and quicker for us to know God than it is to know ourselves. For our soul is so deeply grounded in God, and so endlessly treasured and held, that we can scarcely glimpse it until we first know the creator with whom it is united. And I gaze on my creator with virgin eyes; as if they have never before been opened.

And that my unworthy life is united with such beauty and strength, I can hardly conceive; though where I end, and this glory begins, I know not and stand happy in my unknowing, held by the tree, entranced by the sky, intoxicated with scent, quickened by the grass. I hold out my arms in union and wonder ... for how long I do not know.

27

I awake in my cell with the Angelus bell.

Here is the end of the night watch, and the daily call to prayer for our world. Beyond my cell, the flame-keepers quieten their fires, and apprentices hurry ale and bread into their bellies, in preparation for the day. Inside my cell, on my straw by the altar, my senses are stirred, remembering the night before.

For a moment, I wonder if it was something imagined, and from another world ... I can dream most vivid stories. But the mud on my smock declares an earthly adventure from which I am yet to recover.

I am chill, for the fire has died. I failed in my attention last night, swallowed by the sky and held by the oak ... and a fire dies without attention, as my mother taught me.

'You will watch the fire today, Beatrix - for a fire dies without attention. And you'll get my attention, if it goes out!'

I was the best in our house at lighting fires. I never found it so difficult or a chore. And so I reach for my tinderbox, willing a flame beside me now. I place wood shavings and pine needles in the hearth, good dry kindling. I strike the metal across the flint, and strike well. Sparks are caught in the char cloth which begins to glow. I place it on a bundle of tow and blow it into flame - this miracle, the birth of a fire. I set it with the wood shavings to gather strength, blowing hard, adding small sticks, one by one, which crackle in the morning peace, and begin to smoke and catch.

I drink some ale, tasting the hops, drawing on the sweetness; and when the fire is hearty, I cook some porridge, melting oats.

I stir it a little, I watch the thickening, and wonder if I was wrong to step out into the darkness last night. Was I wrong to leave my cell? Shame has never been hard to find in my being; it has always had a voice, like a lazy Lord of the manor, speaking over everyone ... though less so in recent years. The thought that I have done wrong has always been my first thought... but now, thanks be to God, not my last. Shame does not rule as once it did, it dissolves in the light, with kinder thoughts replacing the old.

And of last night, there can be no shame – only gift and delight to my senses! I walked into glory, where God met me most courteously - though he left me on the ground for a while, beauty and terror quite mixed. But if such adventure is sin, then sin is to be much commended!

And later this day, the wall-menders arrive, to heal the wound in the wall... a most sacred wound.

'We come to restore your wall, Mistress Julian.'

He speaks from behind the curtain.

'And I am glad of it,' I say. 'I am glad of the wound - and glad for the healing, for both serve me.'

'Yes, mistress.'

He does not understand me, poor fellow, and I do not explain.

'So do not let me delay you - but tell me your name under heaven.'

'Carter, Mistress Julian.'

'Then seal me well, Mr Carter.'

'Yes, Mistress Julian, we'll do that, we'll seal you well …though I could not be sealed so.'

'You know this?'

'Oh, not as you are, mistress, no.' I feel he shakes his head, as if he has failed in some manner; as if he is not as holy as me. 'I could not do what you do.'

'Then I am relieved. For if you *were* sealed in, Mr Carter, what calamity for us all! Who would then mend the walls that are smashed by violent men?'

'I suppose that is so.'

'Only those with neither gift nor competence are hidden away by the Lord - for he knows they will not be missed.'

'You pray for us, though,' he replies, half in agreement, but looking for good, and I warm to Mr Carter, there is sweetness in him.

'I do, I do. I pray every day, Mr Carter. And every day I sit with myself in solitude and the friendliness of God, until I am quite dissolved and my soul as transparent as expensive glass … but that does not mend walls.'

'We'll do our best, Mistress Julian.'

'Let us each do that, Mr Carter - it is a good calling. Let us each do our best, for our intentions are everything in God's gentle gaze.'

And so I watch them seal me in, seal me again, enclose me again, stone by stone, grunt by grunt, the heaving and the sweat, the wall mended, the stones restored, the grass going and going and then gone from view, the door closed by Mr Carter and his boy ... but so kindly opened for one beautiful night.

28

'You gave me two children, Julian - but I will keep only one.'

I am surprised at her visit, once again by night; for I know her old and aching limbs, the difficulty of the journey.

'Abbess Lucy!'

'Are you safe?' she asks.

'I am safe, thank you, Abbess … safe because of you … and the grace of God.'

'I hear the wall of this cell was attacked.'

'It is mended now.'

I point to Carter's work, which still looks fresh.

'Did they enter?'

'They did enter, Abbess.'

And the shock of it strikes me again, as if I have not felt it until now; the intrusion of two men into my cell, uninvited - the forcing of their way above my way.

'This is disgraceful, you poor girl.'

'I recover.'

'This cell is in the gift of Carrow Abbey.'

She feels her own authority trampled upon.

237

'I believe the bishop ordered the visit.'

'I believe he did,' she says. 'As he orders many visits now. Times are changing around us Julian, each year a new pain. And in truth, I'm glad I shall not live many more of them.' She looks so frail, so tired. 'But they found nothing?'

I shake my head. 'Only the *Pater Noster*, which you suggested I write. They took it away and I pray they enjoy it.'

The abbess smiles a little; but the smile is strained through the cloth of rage and sorrow.

'The new King Henry has passed a law which changes much, *De heretico comburendo*. You need to know this, Julian.'

'What does it change, Abbess? You must tell me what is changed. I cannot imagine worse than what I behold.'

'There is worse.'

'Am I now a brigand?'

'No, you are not ... you are no brigand, Julian. But it heightens fear which is not a good climate; and takes tolerance away. It is not specific against the Lollards, they are not banned; but they are the target for its harsh arrows.'

'How so?'

'It prohibits the translating and the owning of the Bible in English.'

My eyebrows crease. I cannot understand such a law.

'Why do they feel so ill towards their own language?'

'And it authorises the burning of heretics, Julian.' I am unprepared for this and struck harder.

'Mr Curtgate said this would occur.' I remember his words now; words I had not much listened to, too far away. 'He said this. He said they would start with books but not end there.'

'As they do in Europe, so will we now do here.'

She speaks with resignation and I sit down. I feel suddenly the madness of power. I feel the madness of harsh rules made by one over another, when surely kindness is the way? What ignorant strutting declares such things? Men with glass windows ... but no sense.

'The king's father must turn in his grave,' she says, 'God rest his soul.' We cross ourselves in unison. 'John of Gaunt was a protector of Wyclif and his followers, but he's gone now ... and like dogs after hares, his son chases Lollards into a corner, where he will turn them into torches.'

'But you are no Lollard, Abbess.'

I think of her safety, but she thinks elsewhere.

'I am no Lollard, Julian; not by some way. But no one is served by hatred; by men and women caught by the hair and named as demons. Bookshelves and libraries across our land become a threat, an imagined refuge for blasphemy and corruption. They wish to snoop among the Carrow Abbey manuscripts.'

'They snoop in the abbey?' I am stunned at this. 'They have no right to snoop. You must stop them, you must send them away.'

She raises her eyebrows at me, as if to say 'How?'

'They snooped here, did they not? They arrived one day and smashed down the wall of your anchorhold in order to snoop ... and there was nothing to be done, no redress.'

And now I feel scared; but I must ask the question. 'And my child?'

She sighs and I worry further.

'Your child is safe ...for now.' I feel such relief in my body; I am quite overwhelmed. 'But, as I say, Julian,' – and she holds my stare – 'I can only take one man-uscript; and the other, I return to you.'

She passes the rough pages through the window. I take them from her, somewhat disappointed ... though I hold them differently now. Here is a manuscript which could have me ripped from this place.

'Keep these pages from view,' she says. 'If you must keep them.'

It is my diary which she returns to me, the manuscript you now read. Ah, could that be? I wonder if you exist in another place and some future time, when I am with my Lord? Perhaps I now go mad with such thoughts.

'It might be the better way to burn them,' says the abbess. 'They contains names and thoughts which will serve no one well if found.'

'I will burn it,' I say and quite intend to do so, and I also know I will not.

Though perhaps it is a sin, a vanity of mine? The thought returns. Perhaps I write for myself and away from God? Perhaps I should not write of other people and my thoughts toward them. What is gained and who is edified? Is heaven brought nearer? 'I will definitely burn these words, Abbess.'

'But your visions we will keep,' she says. 'Your *Revelations of Divine Love*, as you name them.'

'For that is what they are, Abbess.'

I feel the need to say this.

'We will keep those, while we can ... as we keep the visions of Catherine of Sienna and others. Such writings are not so rare in Italy, France and the Low Countries.'

Does she put me in my place here - as if my visions are quite common and of no great consequence? I wonder always what other people think. I think too much .... and I think too much of what other people think. It holds me back.

'It seems the task of women these days to bring their visions to the church,' she continues, 'though the church does not much thank them.' I'm not sure the abbess thanks them either.

'I hear stories of Margery Kempe,' I say. 'I hear she is also harassed by the church for her visions.'

The abbess stops when I mention this name.

'We'll not talk of Margery Kempe,' she says. I am startled by her firmness and she sees my surprise. 'She is not a woman to admire, Julian.'

'Oh?'

'What can I say? Oh really! She cries all the time and calls it devotion. Do you know that she always cries?'

'I had heard that ...'

'We cannot be always crying.'

'I suppose ...'

'And she speaks of God in the marriage bed with her.' I have not heard this before.

'She speaks of God in? ...'

'She speaks of God in her marriage bed, yes. That's what she says. And yes, it bears repeating. As if anyone should recount such a thing? She says God demands she kiss his mouth, his head and feet as sweetly as she wishes!'

'She has strong experiences of God. I have heard it called mystical union.'

'She can call it what she likes – she can dress it in a robe and place a mitre on its head! It alters not the unhelpful substance, which I tell my sisters at Carrow - lest they be drawn to such things. No wonder the monks and townspeople of Lynn chase her away and the Bishop of Lincoln and the Archbishop of York question her! No, you will do well to avoid her.'

There is much talk of Mistress Kempe in Norwich; and not all of it kind. Many, like the abbess, are suspicious ... and perhaps I am among them, though my heart goes out to her in some manner. I have been told her story, brave in its way. After enduring fourteen children and a failed beer-brewing business, she reached crisis in her life, as people do ... and found herself saved only by frequent visions of Jesus. She began also to cry, she cries a great deal, loudly and most publicly, in response to the divine passion. It is said she can conjure tears at will ... though whether this is gift, I do not know. Abbess Lucy does not believe so.

'I can't be doing with people crying all the time,' says the abbess. 'We have them at the abbey, the hysterical sort. I encourage them to keep it a private affair.'

'So why is she here in Norwich?'

'It was revealed to her.'

I hear the disdain.

'What was revealed to her?'

'To come to Norwich, in order to visit Richard of Caister, the vicar of St Stephen's. She was to make confession to him and tell him of her many and various revelations. She wonders whether her visions are from God or Satan. She asks herself this question every day, I am told. "I need to know," she says. "Are they from God or Satan?" If she came to see me, I would enlighten her.'

'So she has not been to see you, abbess?'

'No ... I think she prefers the men.'

I wonder if this angers her, as if she has been left out. But Margery is like a rolling wave, crashing over our city.

'After meeting Fr Richard, who would be enough for many - he is not easy - she went then to the Carmelite friar, William Southfield, who gave her time, wise counsel and much prayer - a great deal of prayer, he told me - but she left still seeking. She leaves a trail of exhausted souls in her wake ... sucked dry as a summer stick yet declared unsatisfactory. I wonder if an anxious mind truly desires to be healed.'

'I do hear that she is abused,' I say, for Sara has told me this. 'That the people of Norwich, they throw pieces of wood and dead animals at her.'

'I do not wish to be harsh, Julian ...'

'I believe you may have already been so, Abbess ...' I cannot but smile a little.

'But she almost demands it, she demands such response - confessing her sins three times a day in the market place, begging the mercy of Jesus loudly and with much weeping, then collapsing among the buyers and sellers, in her hair shirt. She makes her sisters a laughing stock!' The Abbess' old body is shaking.

'You think so?'

'And then she claims "Only prophets and saints are mocked. I happily join their company!"'

It is said – I only hear what is said – that she forced her husband John to accept a celibate marriage ... though after fourteen children, they may both have been weary. I grew to enjoy such union with Richard ... not at first, no; but we found our way ... though it all seems so long ago.

'And the pilgrimages!' says Abbess Lucy, with a look of disbelief. She will not let Margery go, though before she did not wish to speak of her. 'Even a pilgrimage to Rome - pursuing her visions in the white robe God told her to wear.'

'She does not hide,' I say, seeking the good. 'And nor does she sit still, this is quite certain. I suppose there is something to admire in these things.'

'Visions must take us to *God*, Julian ... and not to the one who receives them. This is the heart of the matter. And while I can see Mrs Kempe in all this, I see her very clear ... I wonder whether I see God?' Abbess Lucy shakes her head. 'She can neither read nor write, apparently.'

It is as if nothing worse could be said; and it is the end of our conversation about Margery Kempe. We sit in silence for a while.

'Will I not see you again, Abbess Lucy?'

She leans forward.

'It is English visions which place us all in danger; those recorded in English. Those in languages unknown, or those in Latin, they do not disturb so much. So I advise you not to speak of your writing, Julian; and we will not.'

'Is my child not worth my speech, Lucy?' I feel somehow gagged and my child stamped on. 'I believe I was told to write these things for all Christians. And now they are to be secret, hidden away and not mentioned - like grubby words in the market?'

The abbess gives me a look. It is a look I have seen before. I see the straightener appear before me.

'Think of Joseph, Mary and the infant Christ fleeing Herod, Julian. Think of them hiding the boy Jesus. Sometimes all we can do is protect a child, until it is their time. Do you understand me?'

I think of the baby Jesus hidden as they travelled, safely screened from dangerous eyes. I think of my book in the library of Carrow Abbey ...

'I understand you, Abbess. I was perhaps hasty in my sense of hurt.'

'So may God keep us safe,' she says, 'Keep us all safe.'

'Indeed.'

'I will not return here, no; and you know this already, Julian.' She says this firmly. I nod. 'I slowly say goodbye to my body; you see how it wanes and rots with the years.'

'You can still frighten, Abbess.'

'Perhaps as a dead snake frightens.' She laughs a little. 'But it is only appearance, it has no bite.'

'I often feared you in the abbey.'

'Feared me? You seemed always a fearless young woman to me.'

'I believe it was a good fear. You never allowed us to stop at our wounds, which Christian folk can do. Instead, you helped us beyond our wounds, firmly but kindly. Firmly always, and kindly, well – *mostly*!'

We laugh together and then she gathers herself, a little awkward.

'And for my knowing of you, Julian, I thank God – no, truly I do.'

'Oh, I ...'

'Be quiet for a moment, woman, and receive this; for we are nothing if we cannot receive. I remember you as that young widow, ripped from husband and child; so eager to help and so eager to please ... and, as I see now, so eager to learn to write as well. The hours you spent in the scriptorium!'

'The abbey was my heaven then, and my saving.'

'You did not absorb much Latin, Julian; it rather passed you by, despite my efforts.'

'I did not warm to it; it had no home in me.'

'But then truth is found not in learning, but in living; and found in the depths of your heart ...which is where you found it.'

'And sometimes find it still.'

'And that's why God sent you to us ... to wash our dishes, to learn to read ...and to brighten our lives. You brighten lives, Julian, your spirit does this. To meet you is to meet an adventure.' Tears form in my eyes. 'We found the right anchoress for this cell, that is a surety. Sister Ruth offered herself before you, did you know her?'

I shake my head.

'She died before her arrival; a good girl.'

'I never knew ...'

'No, well – what was there to say? Life unfolds. Though many thought you would fail ...'

'Thought I would fail?'

I am hurt by this news.

'Oh yes. Too much of a butterfly, some thought.'

'So how come I am here?'

'Because I believed you would succeed in your calling ... whatever your calling was ... or is. I heard God saying 'Yes' when everyone else said 'No'. And you have blessed this space, Julian.'

'And this space has blessed me. These loving walls – they enfold me.'

I do not wish her to leave.

'Step closer,' she says. I move towards her. She is framed like a picture in Sara's window, a dying abbess.

I stand before her and she takes my bowed head in her hands. She has a firm grip, though it shakes a little. 'Bless you, my child, unto eternity. May the Lord bless and keep you always. Fall fearlessly into his love, and all shall be well.'

She continues to hold me for a moment in the silence; I wish always to be held like this. But then gentle release, her hands letting go and with my eyes still closed, I listen to her move from the window, eased by a helper out into the night and out of my life.

'I wish you safe travel, Abbess Lucy!' I call out, but whether she hears me, I do not know, for her cart is being made ready, it creaks and clanks, and the cart-horse complains in the dark.

The goodbye weighs heavy.

29

I do meet Margery Kempe, despite Abbess Lucy's warnings, and not by choice ... though whether truly we meet, I cannot say, but we speak.

She comes by night to my cell, without notice. She rings the visitor's bell, but I am asleep, tucked beneath the altar and slow to respond, so she rings again. I am trying to wake, I make my way to my stool, wondering who is behind the curtain, but before I can speak, and before I am seated, she rings the bell a third time.

'Greetings, dear soul,' I say, gathering myself. It is chill, the fire is cold. 'You must tell me your name and what brings you?'

'My name is Margery Kempe,' she says. 'You may have heard report of me.'

'Greetings, Margery,' I reply, and try to sound gay. 'And what brings you here at this hour?' She tells me she does not wish to stir the ire of these people, the people of Norwich, who attack her like demons.

I tell her I have heard of her arrival in the city, and wish her a blessed and happy stay with us.

Simon Parke

'I hardly come here to be happy,' she says. 'That is no cause to be chased, and one not easily caught!'

'And so in this quest of yours, whatever it seeks, Father Richard and Father William - they were not sufficient?' I do ask her this, for against them, who am I?

'I need much reassurance,' she says, 'a great deal of reassurance, for my sins are scarlet.'

'Are not all our sins scarlet?'

'Mine more so, Mistress Julian, more scarlet, a great deal more scarlet, you would perhaps not understand ... they are the deepest scarlet.'

'I see.'

'So it is for reassurance that the sweetness of the Lord brings me here.'

'A goodly transport, quite the best.'

'And with whom I have had many holy speeches and conversations. Very many ... we have spoken often ... myself and the Lord.'

'Then you are most blessed.'

'And my revelations, of course ... I have had many and wonderful revelations.'

I find a response difficult, as one seeking footing on a slippery climb. So I leave silence, and into the silence she speaks. She speaks of her life - of compunction, contrition, sweetness and devotion; of compassion with holy meditation and high contemplation ... and of the "many wonderful revelations given".'

'Perhaps you should instruct *me*!' I say, wishing to jest a little, for our moment needs a jest, a little laughter would help this night hour.

'Can we not open the curtain?' she asks.

'It is better we have cloth between us,' I say, 'the better for me to listen. My eyes can leave me tired.'

She does not like the curtain closed, this I sense; though she speaks on, gathering pace.

'But whether these revelations are from God or Satan, Mistress Julian, I cannot know ... and I need to know. This concern will not leave me and I seek an answer, for I find no peace in the matter; I will not be soothed.'

It appears as a challenge.

'You say you cannot know?' I ask, surprised.

'Hence this cruel shirt, Mistress Julian - this most cruel shirt! It is to keep my soul in check and in the deepest contrition.'

'I see.'

'Perhaps you do not wear a shirt like this. I do not judge you and it matters not. Do you wear such a shirt?'

'I do not, no.'

'Neither horse-hair nor thongs of metal?'

'Again, no ... I do not believe they are God's friends.'

'Reminders of our sweet Lord, surely?'

'And nor do I believe our Lord sounds like Satan in his speech, not in any manner.'

'Your voice is weak, Mistress Julian, you must speak up.'

She still seethes about the curtain.

'Forgive me, Margery, I need water. I was simply saying that I do not believe our Lord sounds like Satan in his speech.'

'But how does one know? How can anyone know?' She asks this strongly. 'For was not Eve fooled in the garden by the snake, who sounded most like God?'

'Indeed.'

'And would it not be the most terrible thing if I, like Eve, was fooled and mistook one for the other? I greatly fear this, Mistress Julian ... greatly fear such mistaking.'

And now she begins to cry, I hear her sobs. 'You must not mind my tears,' she says earnestly, as if to reassure me, as if she does not wish for me to be worrying.

'I do not mind them, not at all,' I say. 'Tears can be a godly watering.'

'They are tears of devotion, Mistress Julian, tears of devotion - some do not understand this ... such tears of sweet devotion. I sleep with Christ, this has been permitted, and truly, he ravishes my soul, I am left quite ravished. Do these people not understand how good our God is?'

'Let me pour you some ale, Margery' I say. 'I hear you have come a long way.'

'I come from Lynn, yes. But travel is no matter to me. I stay in Norwich at present, but I do not mind travel. I am on a pilgrimage, this is my life - though abused by my fellow pilgrims, who do not believe a woman should travel alone!'

'You must travel as you will.'

'And I am not made dismal by their scorn, not at all! For was not our Lord whipped cruelly – so why should it not occur unto his followers?'

I rise from my seat, cross the cell and pour some ale into a cup. I then return and pass it through the curtain. She takes it, but not with charm.

'I had hoped you might offer more than ale, Mistress Julian ... though maybe I am too large a soul for you to hold.'

'I don't believe so.'

'I am lately a business woman, Julian - a business woman of some standing, a traveller, a receiver of visions and mother of fourteen children - while you have been, well ... in hiding for many years, and a godly hiding, I'm sure. But have you lived anything beyond this incarceration? This is all I wonder. I wonder if I am too large for you?'

I breathe deeply. I even count on my fingers to five. 'Do your revelations bring peace and calm?' I ask.

'Peace and calm?!'

She seems thrown, as if the tribulations of this world forbid peace and calm.

'For truly, when the Lord appears, peace is received,' I say. 'Yet your tears seem heavy and wretched, Margery.'

'I'm sorry?' She is bemused. 'You speak strangely, for my tears are tears of devotion, I know this to be so.'

'And maybe this is so,' I say, 'maybe this is so ... though they appear to arise more from despair than devotion.'

'Well, I ...!'

'Only you can know, Margery - but your tears seem well filled with fear and shame. Could this be so, dear soul?'

'They are tears of happiness.'

'They sound otherwise.'

And now she cries again, I hear her simper, though slowly, a silence appears.

'I seek only forgiveness, Mistress Julian.'

'With your pleading, and your crying and your shirt of thorns ... yes.'

'Well, we must all seek forgiveness, surely? It is our life-long quest, is it not?'

'Yet you have forgiveness, Margery; you have it already. Why seek what you already possess? You have it a hundred times over, pressed down and running over.'

'For my adultery?' she says, with force 'For my *adultery*?' She pauses. 'And now I shock you, perhaps?'

'You do not shock me.'

'So tell me - do I have forgiveness for my *adultery?*'

She almost snarls the word.

'I wonder only that you need to ask.'

'I have not told Father Richard or Father William of this. I have told no one ... no one ... and I do not know why I tell you now. I startle you, I know that ... though perhaps you best know a little of the world out here. You did not know of my scarlet sin – and now you are silent. Perhaps you reconsider your forgiving words?'

Has she not heard me?

'It is true I did not know of your adultery, Margery.' My throat is suddenly dry, so I drink a little. 'And true also that I do not care ... if you understand me.'

'You do not care?'

'For God does not care, Margery. He cares not at all.'

'Well, *I* think he cares – and will punish!'

'Yet I find no kind of wrath in God, Margery ... neither briefly nor for long - so where is God's concern? It is a great unkindness for you to blame yourself for your sin, since our Lord does not blame you for it!'

'But ...'

'I wonder only that these things still hold you down, when our Lord asks only that you rise up. That you rise up, Margery! That is his only care, that you stop weeping. I see no other care here.'

'It was long ago,' she says, 'Long, long ago ... but it remains an unmoveable stain. And you cannot move it, anchoress. It is for this very reason that I have spoken of my adultery to no one. There is nothing they can do, nothing you can do. What can anyone do?'

'I do not try to move it, Margery, for it is not there. I cannot move what has neither colour nor substance. Yet you have decided upon its shape and weight, and insist on hugging it to your breast like a dead child ... when it is no more, when it is quite gone.'

'Well, I myself have known a dead child! Yes, indeed, you may not be aware! But I have known this and for such reason, I do not find your words helpful! You mean well, I am sure ...'

I keep silence; there is no other way before me. Just silence.

'I hear music,' she says. 'On occasion.'

'Music?'

'A quite heavenly melody, I often hear it, music that could only be from heaven, I believe so, I hear it in my head – and it is so beautiful, it makes me weep and wish for a chaste life, like that of our Lord. Do you believe this to be right, Mistress Julian?'

'A chaste life, Margery ... with a husband?'

'I wear a robe of virgin white for our Lord!'

'And your husband?'

'He understands,' she says.

'Are you exhausted by him?'

'We have known each other much, and I have borne much. I have fourteen children! Fourteen alive ... and three with our Lord.'

'A fine crowd.'

'But now I am ravished by God, and am to be only his – not my husband's, only his!'

'Discerning the spirit of our deeds, Margery, this is our calling ... to know not only what we do, but why we do what we do. I wonder only ...'

'Yes?'

'You have asked me whether your visions are true ... whether they are from the Lord.'

'I wish to know, yes, I seek reassurance or else I am anxious .... I believe they are - but how can one tell? I do not wish to be Eve!'

'I wonder only, and this is my concern - that you have not met more peace along the way, Margery ... for our dear Lord always brings peace.'

'Peace is not for this life, Mistress Julian; not in my knowing. No, we must stay strong for the battle! Stay strong for the fight!'

'And which fight is this?'

'The fight to be worthy of God!'

I pause again, feeling only failure, and some exhaustion.

'I speak from my weakness, Margery, not my strength ... for the only strength I know, and the only worth I know, is the kind holding of God – God our father, in whom we have our being, and God our merciful mother, in whom we are re-made and restored. In such holding there is peace.'

She seems to choke at this talk of God.

'God our mother?'

'Our merciful mother, yes.'

'I hardly see God so!'

'But how could God not be so, Margery? I cannot speak of God otherwise, and that is all I say this night. We shall both sleep a little now, and by all means return with the morning light. But consider your deeds kindly, Margery, always kindly ... falling only into love and mercy, which is the only fall there is.'

30

Mr Curtgate was burned today.

The Lollard's Pit, so-called, is less than a scream from my cell ... I wish it were further. And I do not wish to write of these things, my quill is stubborn in my hand, it was not meant for this. But I will write, even if it is the end of my writing, for he was my friend.

I smell him in death, as I smelled him in life; but I do not confuse the scents. Burnt flesh invades the cell, though the screams have died. They are brief but never forgotten, surely? Killed in his own parish; and so close to his church. Could he see it through the flames?

And like the mother of Jesus at the foot of the cross, I was there in mind and heart with the passion of Mr Curtgate.

They took him some weeks back, making loud mess in church and vestry. I had closed the curtain across the Christ window, but the bishop opened it, reaching through. He had returned ... I seem only to see him in violence, though no doubt on occasion he kneels. He claimed he smelt 'too much of Wyclif here!' His language was cruder; but I have no time for it.

'I smell only incense and prayer,' I say.

'Are we to open your cell again, Mistress Julian - as we did before?' he asks. He is more breathless now, a tiring man, his face red and purple with wine; his skin, translucent and flaking - the strong skin of youth long gone. Like the abbess, the bishop rots; but he rots in a rage. 'Shall we find a Lollard family hiding behind your writing desk? Or a tract beneath the altar?'

My soul is clamped by fear. Beneath the altar is my testament. I have not yet burned it. I must burn it immediately. Why have I not burned it?

'Your men have already taken my *Pater Noster*, your Grace. I do not believe I have anything else to offer you ... except my prayers; and you know you always have those.'

'I keep hearing of visions, Mistress Julian.' He stares ... then coughs a little. 'These rumours of visions persist in Norwich and I wonder at their nature and purpose. I wonder if the devil has you.'

'I did once see a vision, your Grace.'

'Would you like to confess, child?'

'I believe I celebrate rather than confess for I saw a vision of Christ on the cross, as I hope many Christians have.'

'When was this?'

'Many years ago now; I hardly receive such revelations daily! Scripture, sacrament and prayer now suffice.'

'And what did you see – all those years ago? I do not remember it mentioned. You seem damn quiet on the matter.' He is coughing again. 'It wasn't a vision of the bastard Wyclif?'

Has he listened to me? I have spoken already of Christ. Perhaps his listening is particular and narrow.

'I saw blood pouring from our Lord's head, his face blue with pain and the blessed mother of our Lord weeping.'

'Do you write these visions down?'

The abbess was right. It is the book he fears; words neither the church nor the king can control. And suddenly he appears most weak to me, though he lives in a palace, orders men and holds my life in his hands. He, too, is afraid.

'I treasure them in my heart, your Grace; for I was also given their meaning.'

'And what meaning were you given, woman?'

He leans forward in the window, an inquisitor; and blessed by the abbess, I breathe in courage.

'Toward the end of the vision, I was asked: do you want to know what our Lord meant in all this?'

'Yes, yes – *and* ...?'

'I said that surely I did. So then the voice said to me "Know it well, Julian - love is his meaning."'

I pause.

'Love?'

'This is what the voice said, your Grace: he told me that love is his meaning.'

'And is that all?' He appears disappointed.

'Is that not enough?'

'I mean, he said nothing more?'

'There is nothing more to say.'

'This is no vision, woman; it's a rambling born of too much fasting.'

'Remain firm in this love, he said to me, and you will taste it ever more deeply. And I have found this to be so, your Grace - knowing nothing apart from love. And I thank you for this. For this is the adventure you gave me when you allowed me to come to this place.'

The bishop has drawn back a little.

'You always were an odd fish, Mistress Julian. Though pretty enough and much wasted here.'

'So if the good people of Norwich speak of my visions, your Grace - well, I am glad they speak ... though not that they accuse me or assault my cell with burning logs. For nothing that I saw or heard from God stands outside the teaching of Mother Church; but rather, I believe these things strengthen her.'

But the bishop only stares.

'Mr Curtgate possesses Lollard writings. Did you know this?'

'I did not ...I do not. I do not know what Lollards write!'

'Did he share them with you, Julian? Did he creep his way into your anchorite soul, like some rat in a grain store?'

'He showed me nothing but a kind heart and the bread and the wine.'

'He owned an English bible.'

'And burned it for you ... he told me.'

'But not his library ... he did not burn his *English* library.'

'It is the language of the street.'

I cannot help but say it.

'And so a language unworthy of God, woman! Shall the Almighty really be described in the slang of the market place, as though he were a fish or a turnip? Is that fitting?!' I do not respond. He boils suddenly. 'And he will burn for this blasphemy. We can burn the heretic now. Have you heard this good news?'

'Which good news?'

'Thanks to our new King Henry, God bless him, we can drain the swamp of Lollardy at last.'

'If that is the way of love ...'

'Be careful, Julian - or my men will visit again.' I hold his stare. I have little to lose, this sense arises in me; so little to lose ... and my existence is strengthened in this knowing. 'And a woman will burn with Mr Curtgate,' he adds.

I am shocked, so shocked ... and he is pleasured by this, his bulbous eyes dance.

'Who?'

The sudden thought: is it me?

'The fruit seller woman, Morley.'

'Morley?'

'You know her?'

My tone betrays interest and he is the inquisitor again.

'I do not,' I say, and this is not quite a lie. 'I knew her father, I believe ...from visits to the market. I was often sent to buy fruit.'

'Her husband found her out, declared her a "Lollard whore" ... he said she knew Mr Curtgate too well, much too well ... a little nest of vipers, bedding down on tracts against the Pope, tracts against church property. This man turns words into poison! But now this vile nest shall be burned - with Mr Curtgate and Mistress Morley inside.'

I listen with horror. I know of Mistress Morley. The night before he was taken, her name arose in my converse with Mr Curtgate. I was at the Christ window for confession, when he arrived distraught.

'I cannot receive your confession tonight, Mistress Julian.' His long face is lined with worry, his hair greying, his stubble rough. 'I wish you rather to receive mine.'

'I cannot receive a confession, for I am not a priest. You know this, Mr Curtgate.'

'We are all priests,' he says. 'Mr Wyclif speaks truly. I always knew this.'

'Mr Curtgate ...'

I am disturbed.

'And now I must speak it.'

'Speak what?'

'I did meet with a woman for counsel.'

'Which woman?'

'Mistress Morley.'

'This is allowed, I believe ... that you counsel a soul in your care.'

'Not alone, though ... one should never counsel a woman alone. And God forgive me for doing so.'

'She knocked on your door?'

'She knocked on my door and I let her in - because I wished to be alone with her, this is the truth. I wished to be alone with her. I had feelings for Mistress Morley – in a manner. But truly, I thought only to talk.'

'And what did you talk of?'

'She had difficulty with certain beliefs. I remember she questioned transubstantiation, certain religious images ... she prefers the scriptures to ceremony.'

'She follows Mr Wyclif?'

'She says the scriptures are sufficient ... there are these people, Mistress Julian, people of good faith, they are not demons. And she possesses an English bible, which I did warn her of, and quite soundly.'

'I see no need for confession here, Mr Curtgate.'

'When she left me, she thanked me with a kiss.' He pauses ... it seems difficult for him to speak. 'And I returned it.'

'You returned it?'

'Her touch was so gentle, Mistress Julian, I could not help myself. I am a single man, this is no reason, but I do not often feel such touch - and then she returned it once more.' My heart supports them, for I too remember such kisses, such joy ... though so long ago. 'And I felt her body, I held her - not as a priest - before ceasing from my sin.'

'There was no - union?'

'Only of hearts, Mistress Julian, only of hearts; but it was a stained union and against all teaching, I know this.'

'And you hurt yourself with these thoughts, Mr Curtgate? The thoughts of a kiss?'

'She was betrothed to another, betrothed to another ... yet I could not help myself.'

'You did not force yourself upon her?'

'Force myself? No, I did not, no, Mistress Morley felt – well, I do not know what she felt, she had a sense for me, I believe. But it matters not, I am a priest, I should not have allowed such things, a man in holy orders.'

'Though also just a man.'

'A man of clay and quite unworthy. And now I wish my sin to be named, for it will not let me be. It pulls at my hair and spikes my eyes, as though I am already in hell.'

'You will not let yourself be?'

'Let myself be? How can I let myself be? No, I have tested God too far ... and walked manacled ever since.'

I ponder this broken man at my window, tears breaking in his tired eyes.

'You mistake the beginning for the end, Mr Curtgate.'

'I do not follow you.'

'The fall is no test of God's love, but rather, it's birth ... and God is in both. Do you not understand?'

'You say that God is in the fall? Mr Wyclif never said that!'

263

'Jesus spoke it – to me. I follow Jesus, not Mr Wyclif.'

'He said God is in the fall?'

'Of course! Of course God is in the fall! The wound is not the end but the beginning, the door through which Christ enters. Your wound is your crown, Mr Curtgate, if offered to God; for in the cracks and in the sore place, in the painful fall – all given by God - begins the healing of the world.'

'I have not heard such things ...'

'It is not your slip that tests God – but your refusal to get up and go free. From here, you walk as a man un-manacled, a man who is free!'

He seems to relax.

'I did know freedom once,' he says. He looks wistful.

'When did you know freedom?'

'When first I read Mr Wyclif's words; something stirred, Mistress Julian, and hell dimmed a little.'

'Then return to that place of grace, Mr Curtgate. Christ waits for you in your heart, and calls you to join him in your beautiful soul.'

And this was my last conversation with Mr Curtgate, for they came early next morning. Perhaps he knew already of their approach when we spoke. He walked quietly down the aisle when they came, and though tied roughly, he was not manacled - not in any manner, if you understand. He glanced across to the window we have shared, and I do believe he smiled. Had Mr Curtgate allowed himself peace?

And so it was they died together in the Lollard's Pit, Mr Curtgate and Mistress Morley ... close in death, if forced asunder in life.

And now I sit here at the end of this day quite empty. I am quite empty. I ponder the cross on the altar, so long my companion. It does not speak. I am weary of sad goodbyes, of lives cut short – too weary. I have seen too many lost, while I have lived on.

I think of my father, though I have lost his face ... of Richard and Lettice, such faraway folk, but close outside in the ground ... I think of Mr Ball, of Sara, of Peter the cat, of Abbess Lucy ...and call them friends. And the agony of letting go arises in me again, as Christ in his passion let go of all he had been, all he had loved and all that he hoped for. 'My God, my God, why have you abandoned me?'

Is this old age?

The pattern of life changes, does it not? It changes with time, inviting ever deeper surrender into the mist of unknowing and emptiness; and the discovery there of different joy. This I find with the passing of years ... though not today. Not all days are kind.

And as I sit, I remember also my mother, who died shortly after her visit here. The sense of two paths arises in me ... two paths that ran close with each other but never met. I do not think my mother and I ever met, not in our souls.

And as the ashes cool in the Lollard's Pit - the crowd gone home and the pie-sellers rich - I sit beyond both despair and fury. I grab at both, for both are familiar ... but they slip through my fingers, as ghosts who now have no place, their haunting done.

I let go of all that has been, both beauty and pain, blue bells and plague, kindness and violence, as if all are one in twisted majesty. We best make peace with pain and delight, for when the whole world is known, and all revealed ... all will be known to be well.

I let go also of this book, and the writing of it; I need it no more, my writing is done; I cannot imagine another word. I wish now only to be ... and to love. The greatest honour we can give Almighty God is to live gladly in the knowledge of his love, for love is his meaning. I do this on my best days; and on my worst, still know the way home.

And so I arrive at emptiness. In my three-windowed cell – my palace ... it is undoubtedly my palace – I arrive at the emptiness where, God willing, glory may enter.

All shall be well, and all shall be well and all manner of things shall be well, I believe so. This, my dear and future friend, is my testament.

Post script

I, Thomas Bookman, in my own hand, complete this journal by the anchoress, Mistress Julian of the cell by St Julian's church in the grand city of Norwich where she died in the year of our Lord, 1416.

As is the tradition for anchorites, she was taken from the cell and buried in a grave unmarked ... lest people gather there in reverence and look not to their own souls and saviour.

And it was I, Thomas Bookman, who discovered her death – a harsh day. I arrived with food and ale, and found her asleep by the altar, her fire and body grown cold. With allowance from Bishop Alexander and Abbess Rachel of Carrow Abbey, I entered the cell through the window, with two nuns, (they struggled a little) both to clear and to clean.

The vicar of St Julian's, Mr Harvey, arranged for the digging of the grave. On moving the body - so light to lift, as though nothing of her remained - I found her to be holding a wooden boat, skilfully carved. I did not then know why she held it in death, though I have since discovered. But we lay it with her, for she held it tight ... the boat to Sweden.

We found also in her cell this book, named *The Secret Testament of Julian*. It lay in the fire, there to be burned; though, in truth, it was scarcely scarred - placed too late for the flame. Perhaps she did not wish for the flame to have it, I do not know; perhaps she wished to be known, wished to be heard. The nuns who accompanied me did not desire the manuscript. I believe they feared it, and moved away, as if it were a bear. The new bishop likes books less even than the last, and the last was no friend.

And so with joy, I take it for myself, for I like books ... and I loved this woman ... in a manner. And she has bound it well enough – well enough for one not skilled, though my father would find fault ...the leather is a little creased, he would say this, were he alive.

As this manuscript reveals, she stopped writing in the year of our Lord 1406, after the burning of Mr Curtgate and Mistress Morley, which caused her much anguish; though Mr Morley said in the market place that they deserved it. I do not repeat here what he said of his wife.

I now complete this journal only that Julian may be kindly remembered. For when my father's bookshop was ransacked and burned, I was upset and sore in her presence and quite broken. She told me to come to Sara's window, where she greeted me and took my hand.

'Thomas, these are difficult days.'

'They are indeed, mistress.'

'But you are kept, Thomas ... kept safe in God's heart.'

'I know only the storm today.'

'Then know also the calm that holds it. The storm is held in a calm. We are enfolded in a great love.'

And I have remembered her lines, and believe in some manner; though I struggle, for truly, these are the most terrible of times, like none before, when calm and love are well-disguised.

And sometimes I walk by her grave. I make it my path, at the close of the day. It is unmarked land by the oak tree, with no remembrance of her name. There is only a mound, and even this grows hidden with the passing weeks ... though it is close to a headstone marked *Richard and Lettice, of blessed and most-loved memory.* Through the reading of this manuscript - I have read it all - I too seem to know them now, but living not dead, they somehow live ... and I bless them all, this sweet family, on my way, for I have no family left.

And it is not my business, not these days; but I find it strange that another anchoress now lives in her cell, a nun from the abbey, who has also taken the name Julian. So same-named, but not the same ... or not for me.

For she was not Mistress Julian, but Julian of Norwich, this I dare now call her: Julian of Norwich! And here is her testament, her suffering, her kindness and sweet genius, in the year of our Lord, 1416.

I close this book.

*The world is suffused by God, so let the winters
come and go*

Paperbacks also available from White Crow Books

Elsa Barker—*Letters from a Living Dead Man*
ISBN 978-1-907355-83-7

Elsa Barker—*War Letters from the Living Dead Man*
ISBN 978-1-907355-85-1

Elsa Barker—*Last Letters from the Living Dead Man*
ISBN 978-1-907355-87-5

Richard Maurice Bucke—*Cosmic Consciousness*
ISBN 978-1-907355-10-3

Arthur Conan Doyle—*The Edge of the Unknown*
ISBN 978-1-907355-14-1

Arthur Conan Doyle—*The New Revelation*
ISBN 978-1-907355-12-7

Arthur Conan Doyle—*The Vital Message*
ISBN 978-1-907355-13-4

Arthur Conan Doyle with Simon Parke—*Conversations with Arthur Conan Doyle*
ISBN 978-1-907355-80-6

Meister Eckhart with Simon Parke—*Conversations with Meister Eckhart*
ISBN 978-1-907355-18-9

D. D. Home—*Incidents in my Life Part 1*
ISBN 978-1-907355-15-8

Mme. Dunglas Home; edited, with an Introduction, by Sir Arthur Conan Doyle—*D. D. Home: His Life and Mission*
ISBN 978-1-907355-16-5

Edward C. Randall—*Frontiers of the Afterlife*
ISBN 978-1-907355-30-1

Rebecca Ruter Springer—*Intra Muros: My Dream of Heaven*
ISBN 978-1-907355-11-0

Leo Tolstoy, edited by Simon Parke—*Forbidden Words*
ISBN 978-1-907355-00-4

Leo Tolstoy—*A Confession*
ISBN 978-1-907355-24-0

Leo Tolstoy—*The Gospel in Brief*
ISBN 978-1-907355-22-6

Leo Tolstoy—*The Kingdom of God is Within You*
ISBN 978-1-907355-27-1

Leo Tolstoy—*My Religion: What I Believe*
ISBN 978-1-907355-23-3

Leo Tolstoy—*On Life*
ISBN 978-1-907355-91-2

Leo Tolstoy—*Twenty-three Tales*
ISBN 978-1-907355-29-5

Leo Tolstoy—*What is Religion and other writings*
ISBN 978-1-907355-28-8

Leo Tolstoy—*Work While Ye Have the Light*
ISBN 978-1-907355-26-4

Leo Tolstoy—*The Death of Ivan Ilyich*
ISBN 978-1-907661-10-5

Leo Tolstoy—*Resurrection*
ISBN 978-1-907661-09-9

Leo Tolstoy with Simon Parke—*Conversations with Tolstoy*
ISBN 978-1-907355-25-7

Howard Williams with an Introduction by Leo Tolstoy—*The Ethics of Diet: An Anthology of Vegetarian Thought*
ISBN 978-1-907355-21-9

Vincent Van Gogh with Simon Parke—*Conversations with Van Gogh*
ISBN 978-1-907355-95-0

Wolfgang Amadeus Mozart with Simon Parke—*Conversations with Mozart*
ISBN 978-1-907661-38-9

Jesus of Nazareth with Simon Parke—*Conversations with Jesus of Nazareth*
ISBN 978-1-907661-41-9

Thomas à Kempis with Simon Parke—*The Imitation of Christ*
ISBN 978-1-907661-58-7

Julian of Norwich with Simon Parke—*Revelations of Divine Love*
ISBN 978-1-907661-88-4

Allan Kardec—*The Spirits Book*
ISBN 978-1-907355-98-1

Allan Kardec—*The Book on Mediums*
ISBN 978-1-907661-75-4

Emanuel Swedenborg—*Heaven and Hell*
ISBN 978-1-907661-55-6

P.D. Ouspensky—*Tertium Organum: The Third Canon of Thought*
ISBN 978-1-907661-47-1

Dwight Goddard—*A Buddhist Bible*
ISBN 978-1-907661-44-0

Michael Tymn—*The Afterlife Revealed*
ISBN 978-1-970661-90-7

Michael Tymn—*Transcending the Titanic: Beyond Death's Door*
ISBN 978-1-908733-02-3

Guy L. Playfair—*If This Be Magic*
ISBN 978-1-907661-84-6

Guy L. Playfair—*The Flying Cow*
ISBN 978-1-907661-94-5

Guy L. Playfair —*This House is Haunted*
ISBN 978-1-907661-78-5

Carl Wickland, M.D.—*Thirty Years Among the Dead*
ISBN 978-1-907661-72-3

John E. Mack—*Passport to the Cosmos*
ISBN 978-1-907661-81-5

Peter & Elizabeth Fenwick—*The Truth in the Light*
ISBN 978-1-908733-08-5

Erlendur Haraldsson—*Modern Miracles*
ISBN 978-1-908733-25-2

Erlendur Haraldsson—*At the Hour of Death*
ISBN 978-1-908733-27-6

Erlendur Haraldsson—*The Departed Among the Living*
ISBN 978-1-908733-29-0

Brian Inglis—*Science and Parascience*
ISBN 978-1-908733-18-4

Brian Inglis—*Natural and Supernatural: A History of the Paranormal*
ISBN 978-1-908733-20-7

Ernest Holmes—*The Science of Mind*
ISBN 978-1-908733-10-8

Victor & Wendy Zammit —*A Lawyer Presents the Evidence For the Afterlife*
ISBN 978-1-908733-22-1

Casper S. Yost—*Patience Worth: A Psychic Mystery*
ISBN 978-1-908733-06-1

William Usborne Moore—*Glimpses of the Next State*
ISBN 978-1-907661-01-3

William Usborne Moore—*The Voices*
ISBN 978-1-908733-04-7

John W. White—*The Highest State of Consciousness*
ISBN 978-1-908733-31-3

Stafford Betty—*The Imprisoned Splendor*
ISBN 978-1-907661-98-3

Paul Pearsall, Ph.D. —*Super Joy*
ISBN 978-1-908733-16-0

All titles available as eBooks, and selected titles available in Hardback and Audiobook formats from www.whitecrowbooks.com

Lightning Source UK Ltd.
Milton Keynes UK
UKHW010731140520
363167UK00001B/133